SKELETONS OF THE ATCHAFALAYA

SKELETONS OF THE ATCHAFALAYA

•

Kent Conwell

AVALON BOOKS

NEW YORK

Library of Congress Catalog Card Number: 2003093929
ISBN 0-8034-9628-1

Published by Thomas Bouregy & Co., Inc.
160 Madison Avenue, New York, NY 10016

PRINTED IN THE UNITED STATES OF AMERICA
ON ACID-FREE PAPER
BY HADDON CRAFTSMEN, BLOOMSBURG, PENNSYLVANIA

To Ryan and Rhet
and
To my wife, Gayle

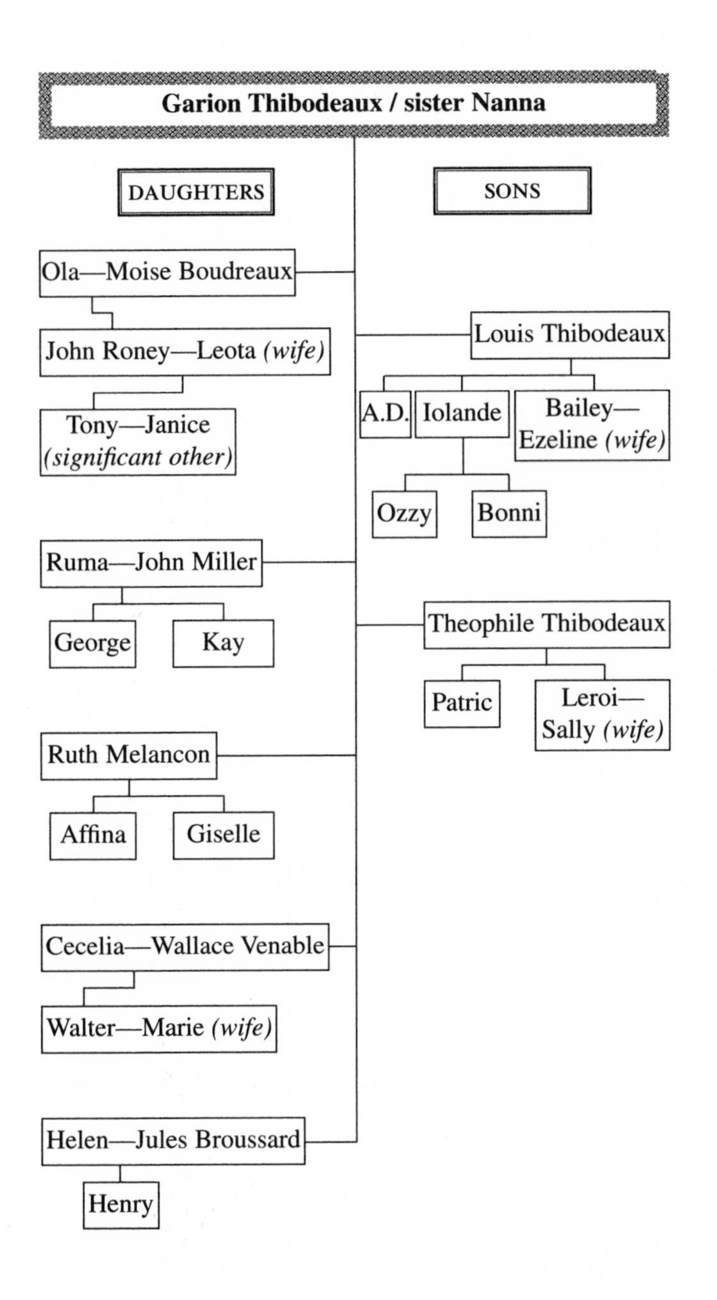
Garion Thibodeaux / sister Nanna
DAUGHTERS
SONS
Ola—Moise Boudreaux
John Roney—Leota (wife)
Tony—Janice (significant other)
Louis Thibodeaux
A.D.
Iolande
Bailey—Ezeline (wife)
Ozzy
Bonni
Ruma—John Miller
George
Kay
Theophile Thibodeaux
Patric
Leroi—Sally (wife)
Ruth Melancon
Affina
Giselle
Cecelia—Wallace Venable
Walter—Marie (wife)
Helen—Jules Broussard
Henry

Chapter One

Our family has a saying that good things happen in threes. However, when we found ourselves in the middle of three deaths within three or so hours of each other with a Category Three hurricane zeroing in on us, I decided that somebody in my family must have been chewing on locoweed.

Every day, with the exception of Thanksgiving and Christmas, 122,000 automobiles speed across the elevated eighteen-mile span of Interstate 10 traversing the Atchafalaya Swamp in Louisiana.

No more than a handful of the occupants of these 122,000 realizes that only thirty feet below there spread two thousand square miles of forest and swamp that time forgot.

The very first time *Grand-pere* Moise drove me down through the giant bald cypress and spreading water oaks in the Atchafalaya, I fell under its spell. Entering that shadowy ecosystem of cypress-tupelo swamps was like stepping back into prehistoric times.

Thirty-two years later, that same fascination still clutches me. Every time I visit the vast swamp, a tingling excitement stirs my blood, but just beneath that exhilaration bubbles a small measure of uneasiness at the primordial unknown that lies beyond the nearest stand of red maple and winged elm.

I've lost track of the number of times I've stepped into a pirogue and within thirty seconds of pushing off from shore, found myself in an antediluvian world in which at any moment I half expected a forty-ton brontosaurus to lift his long neck and tiny head from the brown waters or a savage Tyrannosaurus rex to come crashing through the marshy floodplain with his teeth gnashing.

But not even my wildest imaginings of the chilling phantasmagoria that lurked beyond those lush stands of mixed hardwoods could compare with the bizarre events of our family reunion last June.

Instead of a three-day *fais do do* of food and dancing and laughing over old times, we not only found ourselves cut off from the rest of the world by Belle, a Category Three hurricane, but also confronted with voodoo *wangas,* a family trying to lynch one of its own, and a killer who had decided to double the population of Boudreauxs and Thibodeauxs in the family cemetery. Me included.

The last time I saw Uncle A.D. alive, his fat cheeks and bulbous nose were bright red from the network of tiny capillaries ruptured by too much alcohol, too much rich food, and the mistaken belief he would outlive everyone he had cheated.

When I saw him an hour and a half later, he was dead, lying in a pool of his own blood, a screwdriver buried to the hilt in the side of his fat neck.

To make matters worse, the white members of our family had decided that the killer was its single black member, my cousin, Leroi Thibodeaux.

Since February, I'd been looking forward to the family reunion at Whiskey Bend in the Atchafalaya Swamp. Once every five or six years, someone in the family usually organized a *fais do do*, pronounced "fay dough dough." *Fais do do* is a Cajun corruption of the French expression *faites-le dormir*, literally meaning "make some sleep."

For generations, Cajun families had been coming together for three days of laughter, dancing, and food. They threw pallets on the floor to make some sleep for the youngsters while the adults danced and gossiped and caught up on all the family news.

At first, I wouldn't admit even to myself that something more fueled my anticipation than simply the opportunity to visit family members I hadn't seen in a few years. As I drew nearer Whiskey Bend, I finally acknowledged my ulterior motive for attending the reunion.

After crossing the Sabine River on Interstate 10, I pulled into the Louisiana Highway Tourist Information and Rest Stop. I stepped out for a breath of refreshing Louisiana air. Instead of a clean, cooling breeze, however, a deathly calm and suffocating humidity enveloped me.

I glanced southward, toward the Gulf of Mexico. At that moment, the newscaster on the radio announced that a small tropical disturbance had formed in the Gulf. I grimaced, but shrugged it off. Those who live along the Gulf coast are always facing tropical storms.

The inhabitants have accommodated themselves to deluges, flash floods, and rising tides. With casual aplomb, they shrug off the hosts of snakes, possums, bobcats, coyotes, hybrid wolves, and Florida panthers seeking refuge from the rising water. The water is one of the main reasons so many of the older homes were constructed on piers.

A five-foot alligator emerging from under a house after a storm was not an unusual sight, nor was a water snake nosing around at the front screen, seeking dry shelter. Even the black bears in Atchafalaya headed for higher ground when the storms blew in.

As usual, traffic was heavy on I-10. As usual, the Louisiana Department of Transportation had shut down half the lanes between the Sabine River and Atchafalaya Swamp to accommodate its constant, ongoing construction. And as usual, the Louisiana drivers practiced the philosophy that any speed under eighty was for old ladies and one-eyed widowers.

My on-again, off-again significant other, Janice Coffman-Morrison, had agreed to meet me at Whiskey Bend, the location of the reunion. She'd been judging competition at a daylily show in New Orleans and was returning to Austin. When you're rich—very rich—you can do that sort of thing.

The real reason I was so eager for this reunion was not so much to renew family ties as to show off before my family, most of whom would have given odds that I would end up a bum like my father, John Roney Boudreaux, who deserted us thirty-two years ago when I was seven.

They were wrong. I wanted them to know they were wrong. I wanted them to know that I was a successful private investigator with a Texas license, and that I was a close friend with the heiress to one of the largest fortunes in the state. I didn't plan on revealing it was the Chalk Hills Distillery fortune, although that would certainly endear Janice to the drunks in my family. On the other hand, such an announcement would undoubtedly alienate the women in our family.

Bottom line was that I wanted them to know I was somebody.

That might seem shallow, crass, self-serving. So what? For years, family members watched as I bounced from job to job, smug in their satisfaction that it was just a matter of time until I took off for the anonymity of the road. It was in my blood, some whispered. Like father, like son, others predicted.

But I had proven them wrong, and I wanted them to know it. I glanced at the alligator boots on my feet, a deliberate and expensive purchase aimed at showing them how wrong they were.

* * *

Whiskey Bend is a small village on an island in the middle of the Atchafalaya Swamp, connected to the mainland by a two-mile bridge built back in the administration of Huey Long. I couldn't help noticing the rust on the bridge and thinking to myself that the state was going to have a job on its hands when it started refurbishing the narrow span.

I looked ahead to the end of the bridge, noting the water oak and cypress on either side. A surge of anticipation rushed through my veins. From as early as I could remember, my grandfather and I had made a game of who could see my great-grandfather's house first.

Patches of locoweed, its tiny white flowers forming an umbrella that bobbed up and down with the breeze, grew on the marshy spits projecting out from the island. Every time I saw the plant I remembered the time my cousin Giselle kept our cousin Ozzy from eating one of the pods. "Just because it smells like carrots doesn't mean it's good, dumbbell," she had admonished him.

With a chuckle, I remembered the several times we kids spotted black bears roaming the island. All of us except Giselle had raced for the sanctuary of the big house. And to further enhance her preeminence in our generation, Giselle was the only one of us whoever mastered the whiplike skill of popping the head off a snake.

At the end of the bridge, the water oak and cypress grew thick, blocking a view of the three-story antebellum-styled house.

When I used to drive over the bridge with Grandpa, I always jammed my nose against the windshield to get the first glimpse between two ancient water oaks, the only spot in the stand of trees through which the house could be seen.

Nostalgia washed over me when I reached the end of the bridge. I leaned forward and spotted my great-grandfather's three-story house. "I see it, Grandpa," I muttered, remembering how the old man had taken my own pa's place in raising me.

I braked my pickup to a halt to savor the nostalgia of returning to a part of my childhood. The red brick house sat on a stone and concrete foundation that raised it twelve feet above the ground. Covered verandas surrounded the perimeter of the house on each of the three floors.

With a chuckle, I remembered playing hide-and-seek in the house, especially upstairs where there were four bedrooms on the second floor and five on the third, each with its own fireplace.

Remodeled by my uncle, A.D. Thibodeaux, Great-Grandfather Garion Thibodeaux's house perched on the highest elevation on the island, itself a rough square about three miles on each side. Beyond the house a couple miles was Whiskey Bend, a small community of about 400, the majority of whom were shrimpers or offshore roughnecks.

A crowd milled about on the south and west sides of the house. Cars and pickups were parked at random on the north and east side. Everywhere. I whistled softly when I saw them. At least fifteen or twenty. "What did you expect, Tony?" I muttered. "Eight to ten families, four or five generations each."

According to what Mother had told me over the phone earlier, over sixty family members had attended the last reunion. They expected more for this one. Considering the fact that my great-grandfather had five daughters and two sons, the anticipated attendance did not surprise me.

I pulled up at the edge of the parking area. I didn't want my truck dinged. My pickup was still new, a Chevrolet Silverado. It was a gift from Joe Vaster. He's an east-coast mobster—I mean businessman—for whom I once did a favor over in Galveston.

A brown-haired woman about my age and about half-a-dozen children suddenly appeared between two vehicles. The woman and I stared at each other a moment. Then I recognized her. Giselle—Giselle Melancon. My cousin. I waved through the window and then pulled in beside a yellow and red pickup. I grinned when I saw the logo on the pickup door: Catfish Lube. That meant Leroi was around.

Giselle said something to the children, who raced back to the house. She was waiting for me when I climbed out of the truck. We hugged. "You look wonderful, Tony."

"You too, Giselle. Haven't changed a bit."

She laughed softly and jabbed a finger in her waist, which was thicker than last time I had seen her. She wore loose-fitting denim shorts and a red tank top. "I'm starting to get up there, Tony." She patted my belly. "You're staying trim."

I hugged her around the shoulder and headed for the others. "Try to."

She slipped her arm around my waist.

Nodding to the Catfish Lube logo on the yellow pickup next to mine, I said. "Leroi's here, I see."

She glanced up at me, a look of pain in her eyes. "Yeah. He brought his wife."

"What about his kids?"

She shrugged. "You know kids. The oldest has a car. He and his girlfriend stayed a few minutes and left."

Her tone cooled my laughter. I glanced down at her. "Things any different?"

"What do you think?" She shook her head. "I'm surprised Leroi's still here. He told me he was just going to pop in and out to satisfy his papa."

I grimaced. "Some family we got, Giselle. They hold it against the kid because his father married a black girl. Go figure."

"Yeah, but he's the reminder."

"Yeah. Bunch of bigots. Family or not."

She laughed and squeezed me. "You were always the contrary one, Tony."

"Maybe so." I laughed. "But not this time. A.D. can

drink all he wants. Bailey can brag all he wants. Patric can fight all he wants. Anyone can do whatever they want. I'm just going to smile and agree with everybody."

"Even Nanna?"

I rolled my eyes. "You're kidding. I thought she died."

Nanna was the oldest of the clan, Great-Grandpa's sister. Some family members claimed she was a Seer. I knew for a fact that people went to her for *gris-gris* or *wangas*—all that voodoo nonsense.

"No. She's still alive and kicking."

"How's Affina? She here?"

Giselle grew somber. "Mama had to work. You know she doesn't like these things. Too many memories."

For a moment, there was an awkwardness between us. Giselle's mother, Affina, had never married. The non-event and its subsequent result was one of those old family skeletons hidden away in the back of a closet. I leaned over and kissed Giselle on the forehead. "Well, I'm glad you're here. Tell her I said hi."

"Tony!"

I looked around. A man about my age waved from the porch. His grin revealed brilliant white teeth contrasting with his *café-au-lait* complexion. Next to him stood his wife, Sally.

I waved back. "Leroi!"

Several young children raced past, laughing and shouting. I spotted two or three with tiny flannel bags pinned to their shirts. *Gris-gris*. I laughed to myself. Yep, Nanna was here. She had made *gris-gris* for me when I was a kid.

Leroi led Sally down the steps two at a time. "You old son-of-a-gun," he shouted.

We threw our arms around each other and laughed. After a moment, we reached out and drew Sally and Giselle into our little huddle.

I stepped back and eyed my cousin and his wife. "How long you two been here?"

"Not long. Planned on just stopping in so Pa wouldn't

fuss so much," he replied, nodding to his father, who stood by washtubs full of iced-down beer. Beyond were tables laden with succulent barbeques, spicy gumbos, piquant Creole jambalayas, peppery etouffees, juicy crabs, boiled shrimp, tangy potato salads, dirty rice—just about every imaginable dish in Cajun cuisine.

I frowned when I saw the group Leroi's pa was joshing with. My uncles—A.D., the rich braggart; his brother, Bailey; their cousins, George and Walter; Patric, Leroi's pa; and my cousin, Idiot Ozzy, A.D.'s boy. There was another old man standing with them, his back to us.

A fresh gust of wind swept across the open water, blowing over a few lawn chairs and lifting paper plates from the tables heaped with food and desserts.

Sally spoke up. "Someone said there's a storm out in the Gulf of Mexico."

"I heard it on the radio. Just a small one," I replied, glancing back at the small cluster of men around A.D.

A.D. slapped a hand on the old man's shoulder and leaned over to say something. The man nodded. They both turned and headed directly for us. A.D.'s boy, Ozzy, tagged after them.

My mouth dropped open.

Leroi elbowed me. "Hey, isn't that your old man?"

Giselle pressed her hand to her lips.

"Yeah," I muttered, staring at the approaching figure of John Roney Boudreaux, the father who had deserted Mom and me thirty-two years ago, the same old man who, just a year earlier, I'd found homeless on the streets of Austin, Texas, and taken into my home. He had repaid me by stealing my camera, my sheepskin-lined leather coat, and a few other items to hock.

Chapter Two

Clouds raced across the sun, dragging shadows over the island of Whiskey Bend. From up on the veranda, Nanna's frail voice drifted down to us. "*Ils sont dechire ce soir.*"

I could make out the first two words, "they be" but my command of the Cajun patois was sadly wanting.

Leroi whispered in my ear. "You know your pa was coming?"

I glanced at Leroi. "What do you think?"

"They're heading this way," Giselle mumbled under her breath.

A.D., as usual, bellowed at the top of his lungs. His grin broadened when he spotted us. "John. Over there. There's your boy."

The two of them jerked to a halt a few feet away. A.D. swayed unsteadily. He was feeling no pain, and Pa was drunk, which didn't surprise me. Unable to focus his eyes, he blinked at us and slurred his words. "Where? Which one?"

A.D. thought the question hilarious. He roared. "Why, the light-complected one, naturally." Behind him, Ozzy sneered.

Pa just stared. Obviously, he only had a few brain cells remaining, and even they were probably suspect.

I figured I ought to say something. "Hello, Pa."

He blinked again and grunted, never acknowledging me. "Come on, A.D. I'm going to teach you how to play poker."

"Sure you are, John." A.D. winked at me. "You doing anything now, Tony? Or you still just knocking around?" He jammed a fat hand into his pocket and pulled out a wad of bills held together by a money clip with the initials A.D.T, Adolphus Doudou Thibodeaux, encrusted in diamonds. He waved it under my nose. "You come see me, Tony, and I'll show you how to make this kind of money."

I wanted to tell him what he could do with that wad of bills, but I remembered my vow to be pleasant. I smiled. "Thanks, A.D. I'll keep that in mind."

He glanced at my feet. "Hey, good looking boots."

"Thanks."

He held out his foot. "Mine's ostrich. Four hundred bucks."

"Nice. Mine's Australian saltwater crocodile. Five hundred bucks." I had no idea where the alligator hide came from, probably right here in the Atchafalaya, and they only cost three hundred, but I could play the one-up game as well as A.D.

He cut his eyes at Leroi, and his thick lips twisted into a sneer. With a grunt, he lurched forward, his bulk carrying Pa along with him. They staggered up the dozen or so steps to the veranda and disappeared through the open French doors, but not before Pa called out loud enough for the whole island to hear. "And don't you do no cheating this time, A.D. I'll break your neck if you do."

The four of us looked at each other. "Uncle John didn't even say hi to you," observed Leroi.

I scratched my head. "Truth is, he probably didn't even recognize me."

We all laughed.

"Things don't change much," Sally said.

Giselle replied, her voice a mere whisper. "No, they

don't. They never do in this family." She nudged me with her elbow. "Look, there's your mother."

Mom and Grandma Ola were sitting in white wicker chairs up on the broad veranda, sipping lemonade and becoming reacquainted with the family. "Excuse me, folks," I said to my cousins. "I want to say hi."

Mom wore her usual blue gingham dress with a narrow matching belt. She had not gained a pound for the last forty years. Grandma Ola was half a head shorter, a roly-poly ball of laughter and naughtiness with a penchant for gossip.

I took the steps two at a time. Mom hugged me and wiped the tears from her eyes as I hugged Grandma. "You see your father?" Mom asked.

"Barely," I replied.

In her next breath, she dropped a bombshell on me. "He wants to come home. He wants us to take him back."

Grandma Ola sniffed. "I tell your mother she is crazy to even think such a thing."

Ignoring Grandma Ola, Mom looked up at me, a tiny frown wrinkling her forehead. "What you think, Tony?"

Words failed me. No, words didn't fail me. My brain failed me. It was blank. Pa? My pa? That drunken, lying thief? There was no way I wanted him around, but before I could utter a single word, Aunt Marie Venable swept down on us like a hawk. "Leota. You look wonderful, *Cher*."

Mom rolled her eyes. I nodded, reluctantly disengaging myself from the debate over Pa's coming back home. Still, I had three days. Time enough to take Mom aside and point out the hundred reasons not to take him back.

For the next thirty minutes or so, I waded through a sea of boisterous nephews and nieces, smiling cousins, laughing aunts and uncles. I lost track of all the Broussards, the Millers, the Venables, the Thibodeauxs, and the Melancons. But I made it around to all of them, those down under the trees on the lawn and those in the cool shadows of the verandas that encircled each of the three floors. I paused in the kitchen to grab a slice of ham and make a sandwich with Aunt Iolande and sip some tea with Cousin Kay, all the while trying to sort my feelings about Mom's announcement.

I hated leaving Leroi and Sally alone, but Giselle was with them, and from the veranda, I noticed that some of the Thibodeaux and Miller clans had joined the three.

Aunt Iolande came up to stand beside me in the front entrance as I gazed with nostalgia at the familiar interior of the old mansion I had known since I was a child. Directly in front of me was the grand staircase. To the right of the stairs were the library and kitchen. Just before the kitchen was the open dining area where we children were never allowed to play.

To my left was the living area, and adjoining it in the far corner of the first floor was the parlor, a small intimate room easily heated, and consequently widely used in the colder months.

In her black jeans and white blouse with the ruffled collar, Aunt Iolande looked twenty years younger than her sixty-something age. She wore her hair in a neatly coiffed bouffant despite the fact that the style was fifty years out of date. Maybe there was a fountain of youth somewhere in the single life. "A.D., he make this old house right pretty, don't you think so, Tony?"

She was right. I hated to admit it, but Uncle A.D. had done a fine job restoring the old mansion. The floors were hand-crafted center-cut pine planks polished to a high luster, and the furniture was Victorian cherry wood. The focal point of the living area was the glittering crystal chandelier suspended from the thirty-foot ceiling by what appeared to be velvet ropes that disappeared into a glittering silver bubble on the ceiling, and then emerged from the bubble to drape down to a silver cleat fastened to the wall next to the liquor credenza in the dining area.

When she saw me eyeing the ropes, Iolande explained. "That way, they can lower the chandelier if they gots to.

A.D., he wants it just like it was when Garion Thibodeaux, he buy house."

"Impressive," I replied. And it was.

"A.D., he want that there chandelier to be right over the bottom of the stairs. He say it that way in the picture show, *Gone With the Wind.*"

All I remembered about the stairs in *Gone With the Wind* was that Rhett carried Scarlet up them. But, if A.D. proclaimed there was a chandelier above, who was I to argue?

My cell phone rang. I excused myself and stepped out on the veranda. It was Janice. Her little Miata convertible had broken down just before the eastern entrance to the eighteen-mile elevated span of the Interstate across the swamp.

"Don't worry. I'll be there in less than thirty minutes." After hanging up, I gazed out across the bay. The first-floor veranda being twelve or so feet above the ground, I could see a fair distance across the waters that were growing choppy.

I told Leroi about Janice. "You want to ride with me?"

He hesitated, looking down at Sally. She smiled up at him. "I'll be fine here with Giselle."

Giselle nodded emphatically. "Sure she will. You boys go on. Just be careful."

Leroi pointed to the house. "I've got to make a stop in there first. Too much beer."

"Meet you at my truck. I parked next to you." I hesitated, then detoured by the washtubs and grabbed a couple cold sodas, then a third one for Janice. That's me, always thoughtful, the consummate gentleman who lets his genteel lady drink from a soda bottle. On a table under a nearby oak sat a collection of fruit jars filled with a clear liquid. With a shrug, I grabbed a pint jar.

Uncle Bailey arched an eyebrow. I patted my stomach. "Nowhere but Louisiana," I replied.

He laughed. I never could figure out why, but all you

had to say to make Uncle Bailey laugh was repeat those words, "Nowhere but Louisiana."

Leroi and I roared across the two-mile bridge. He took a large swallow from the jar and handed it to me. I hesitated, then rationalized. What the heck. One can't hurt. But guilt was playing havoc with my conscience. I glanced sidelong at Leroi and turned up the jug. Instead of a large gulp, I barely sipped it. We popped open our sodas. I took one sip and stuck mine between my legs.

Leroi scooted around in the seat and looked straight at me. "You got no idea how good it is to see you, Cuz. I was planning on leaving, but now I'm looking forward to three days of family fun."

I discovered when we returned that not even in Cajun Louisiana do they spell the word fun, M-U-R-D-E-R.

Chapter Three

At I-10, we cut east.

Leroi patted the dashboard. "Nice truck." A gust of wind slammed into us, causing the truck to swerve. "Whoa," Leroi exclaimed, glancing in the direction of the Gulf. "Getting strong."

The concrete bridge was even with the treetops, which were swaying in the gusts. "Yeah. You look like you're doing okay in the lube business. What's that Dodge you're driving, a 2500?"

He sipped the beer. "Yeah. I bought it when I opened the fourth shop."

I whistled, truly impressed. "Four? I didn't know about the last two."

With a sheepish grin, he replied, "Yep, I'm a chain now. A small one, but Catfish Lube has four locations in Opelousas. Getting ready to expand to Lafayette next year."

"You don't mean it?" I looked at him in surprise. "Sounds like you're doing great, man."

He shrugged. "Well, I'm trying. It gets a little tough now and then."

I failed to catch the nuance in his tone. "Where'd you come up with a name like that, Catfish Lube?"

Leroi laughed. "Name of the town, Opelousas. You know, like the catfish. How about you?"

I brought him up to date. He already knew about the brief career I had teaching English to kids who didn't want to learn in schools that didn't want teachers to teach or administrators to discipline. It was always a toss-up whether you would leave school each afternoon in your car or in an ambulance.

"Then I tried insurance. That was a bust. Of course, that's where I met Janice, the one we're going to pick up. I helped her out of an insurance jam. Neither of us were interested in getting serious, but we have fun together." I chuckled and took a sip of soda. "She's rich, too rich for someone like me. I'm just a dependable escort and confidant."

Leroi arched an eyebrow. "Sounds intriguing."

"Not really. We're good friends, and we like being with each other."

"Ummm. And that's it?"

I glanced at him, picking up the suggestive tone in his question. "You know me, Cuz. I never kiss and tell."

We both laughed.

A wrecker out of Lafayette was hooking up to the Miata when we drove up. Janice waved. With her other hand, she held her hair to keep the gusty wind from whipping it into her eyes. She hugged me.

I introduced her to Leroi. "You've heard me talk about Leroi."

She looked from me to him and back, clearly puzzled, but too much of a lady to ask the question on her mind.

I played innocent. "My cousin. Remember?"

"Your—your cousin?"

Leroi stepped forward and offered his hand. "I'm the one nobody wants to talk about." He laughed. "You know, the black sheep in the family."

Janice cut her eyes toward me in surprise, then reasserted her self-control and took his hand. "Well, I'm very pleased to meet you, Leroi." She shot me a dirty look. "The truth is, Tony didn't tell me everything about you."

Leroi laughed again. "He never tells anybody the whole truth, Janice. After thirty-eight years, I've become accustomed to that."

The wrecker driver climbed out of his truck and strode back to us. "I'm ready to go, Miss Morrison. I—"

"Coffman-Morrison." She corrected him.

He rolled his eyes. "Coffman-Morrison. There ain't no dealer in Lafayette for these little things. You know where you want me to take it?"

Leroi spoke up. "Beauchamp Motors is a dependable place." He looked to the driver for agreement.

The driver shrugged. "Hey, Beauchamp's good. Expensive, but they stand behind their work."

Janice nodded. "That's it then."

A strong gust of wind whipped across the bridge, carrying with it a few drops of rain. The driver nodded in the direction of the Gulf. "You folks best get along. I just heard over the radio the storm has turned into a hurricane. Belle, they're naming her."

Once off the bridge and down among the trees, the wind was not as noticeable, but according to the radio, the storm was intensifying. Janice looked up at me. "How bad is it?"

"Not as bad as it looks." I grinned at her.

Leroi chimed in. "Yeah. We get stuff like this two or three times a year."

When we hit the two-mile bridge, I saw the water had risen almost a foot with the tide. I said nothing, just hoping the family had started to evacuate.

Outside, trees swayed in every direction. Patches of rain crashed against the windows. Then just as suddenly as it started, the wind let up and the rain ceased. Moments later, the cycle repeated itself, each time the duration and intensity of the rain and wind increasing.

"Hey, look at that idiot," Leroi shouted, pointing to a

towboat attempting to push a barge through the three-foot waves.

"Where's he going?" Janice leaned forward.

"Probably trying to make port before the storm hits."

Leroi shook his head. "He's in big trouble."

"We can't worry about him," I said, pushing the pickup as fast as I dared. "Let's just get back and get everyone out."

A frown knit Leroi's forehead. "I wonder why we haven't met some coming out already. Everything outside has got to be soaked by now."

I hadn't voiced my own concern, but that very fact was worrying me as well.

Just before we reached the end of the bridge, the entire structure shuddered.

Leroi looked around. "What was that?"

I glanced in the side mirror. "Beats me."

"Hey," Leroi shouted, looking out the back window. "The barge! It hit the bridge."

I was too busy watching the two lanes ahead of me between gusts of blinding rain to worry about the barge.

"Look at that," muttered Leroi, turning back to the front. "There's nobody out by the cars. You think they plan on riding it out?"

Without warning, the rain ceased.

"Is it over?" Janice looked up at me.

"No. It comes in spurts. Bands of rain are caught up in the circulation. The closer to the eye, the more intense and constant the rain is."

"Not counting the wind," Leroi added with a wry laugh.

As we reached the end of the bridge, a car passed us heading out. It was Uncle Henry Broussard. He was alone. I waved for him to stop, to tell him to look out for possible damage to the bridge, but he ignored me.

When we came within sight of the old mansion, Janice caught her breath. "Tony, it's beautiful. Just like some I've seen along River Road near New Orleans."

A sense of pride welled up in my chest. Leroi and I grinned at each other. "It's old. Built before the Civil War. Great-Grandfather Thibodeaux bought it back in the 1920s according to my mother. Grandma claims he got his money by bootlegging. The first floor is actually about ten or twelve feet above ground. Underneath is open storage. In the old days, that's where the kitchen and dining areas for field hands were. We always heard there were secret passages in the old house."

Leroi chuckled. "Yeah, but we never found any. And we looked."

"Yeah. We sure did."

"Hey, remember the games of hide-and-seek we'd play? And hey, remember how we used to hide secret messages in the clean-out bin in the fireplace in the library?"

I grinned as memories of some of those carefree days at Whiskey Bend came back to me. "Yeah. And remember the time we left Ozzy down under the house and he got scared?"

Janice looked up at me. "Ozzy?"

"Osmond Thibodeaux," Leroi replied.

"Our cousin," I explained.

"The real black sheep in the family," Leroi said, laughing. I joined in.

The grounds around the house were empty except for overturned chairs and tables. I parked close to the front steps.

Family members on the veranda turned to look at us.

"Looks like something's going on inside," Leroi said.

Bailey Thibodeaux stood on the veranda, his thin hair plastered to his head by the rain. Hands clenched into fists, he stood nose to nose with Patric Thibodeaux. When he spotted my pickup, he jabbed a finger at us. "There he is. Down there," I could hear him say.

Patric grabbed at his shoulder, but Bailey shook his cousin's hand off and stumbled down the steps, followed by three or four other men, Osmond Thibodeaux among them. The grin on my face vanished when I saw the rage contorting theirs. They yanked the passenger door open and jerked Leroi from the pickup.

"He's the one," a voice shouted. Ozzy Thibodeaux threw a wild punch that missed Leroi by a foot. Janice cringed against me.

"Someone get a rope," another yelled.

Another voice called for reason.

I crawled over Janice and tumbled out the door. "Stop it," I shouted, jumping to my feet and pushing one of my uncles away from Leroi.

A general pushing, shoving match took place as more family members crowded around, shouting obscenities and oaths. Several fights broke out among them.

Grumbling under my breath, I fumbled in the glove compartment. I jerked my .38 out, and in a move reminiscent of the old West, fired three shots into the air.

Everyone froze.

I pulled Leroi behind me. "Now what are you idiots up to? What's going on?"

Bailey, his shirt hanging open to reveal his protruding belly, pointed at Leroi. Gasping for breath, he snarled. "I'll tell you what's going on. He killed my brother. He killed A.D."

"What are you talking about?" I asked, confused.

"We found A.D. dead upstairs, stabbed with a screwdriver."

"Yeah. He killed my pa," shouted Ozzy, pushing forward. "And we're going to get him for it."

I shoved him back. "Leroi was with me. He couldn't have done it."

"I saw him go upstairs," Ozzy said, jabbing a finger at Leroi. "Before you two left, he went upstairs."

Leroi pushed around me. "So what? I had to use the bathroom."

Someone snorted. "I bet."

From the rear of the crowd, another voice shouted. "Lynch him."

Patric, Leroi's father, spun and fixed his eyes on the agitator. He wrinkled his button nose until it was almost flat against his face. "You try that, George, and I'll wrap that rope around your scrawny neck."

"Hanging's a good idea," shouted Ozzy, who was a couple years older than me, but he'd been spoiled by his daddy. I put my hand on his chest and shoved him back. "Shut your mouth, Ozzy. You're not going to do a thing, and you know it." About then I wished Giselle had not stopped him from eating that locoweed years earlier. Or maybe that was his problem. He had ingested a touch of it, and it addled him.

He grimaced, but remained silent.

Bailey shouted. "Lynching is better than he deserves. We ought to—"

I shouted, "Shut your mouth, Uncle Bailey."

He looked at me in surprise.

"And shut it now," I added.

Bailey glared at me. He snorted. "I heard you was some kind of private eye or something. You got no jurisdiction here."

I eyed the crowd. It's amazing how anger can so twist a face that you can't recognize it. "You're right, Bailey. I've got no jurisdiction, but you aren't the law either. What we need to do is call the police. What about Whiskey Bend? Is there a constable?"

"No." George Miller stepped forward. A shrimper, he was short and wiry, his sun-blackened face filled with wrinkles caused by squinting into the sun. "We use the state police."

"Then that's who we need to call."

"We tried, but the line's down. Henry went to get them."

Walter Venable spoke up. "Phone went out when the electricity went out."

I noted the lights in the house. "Looks like there's electricity now."

Iolande, A.D.'s sister, spoke up. "A.D., he put a generator in the shed. Fixed it to go on when the power went off."

"There's lights, all right, but the TV's garbled. Can't make nothing from it," Uncle George said. "Radio works so far."

"Who has cell phones?"

Three had them. Naturally, they couldn't reach their server. So much for the luck of the Boudreauxs.

I studied the crowd a moment. "All right, folks. Let's go back inside. I—"

"What about him?" Ozzy pointed to Leroi.

With a sigh of frustration, I shook my head. "What about him, Ozzy? You think he's going to run away?" I blew through my lips. "After all these years, you aren't any smarter, just uglier. He isn't going anywhere. Now just back off." I addressed the crowd again. "I've got a laptop and cell phone. Maybe my phone will work. We can contact the state police. We'll get them out here."

A voice sounded from the rear of the crowd. "Won't do no good."

I looked around.

Uncle Henry pushed through the crowd and nodded to the bridge. "We're stranded."

"Stranded? What do you mean?"

"Yep. Barge hit the bridge. Knocked a ten-foot span out. Two minutes sooner, and I'd of been across."

Taking a deep breath, I considered the situation. Right now, these folks were not family, they were a mob. I had to settle them down. "All right. The bridge is out. That means no one can come in or go out. Whoever did this can't get away."

Ozzy jabbed his finger at Leroi and shouted. "He did it. It was his screwdriver."

I shouted back. "Shut up, Ozzy. You got no proof. None

of you." I glared at them. "We're family here. Not a mob." Another band of rain hit, even more intense this time. By now, we were all soaked.

George Miller blew through his lips. "You right, Tony." He stepped forward and took Leroi's hand. "Me, I'm sorry, Leroi. Tony, he right. We got no proof." He glanced around at those behind him. "Any one of us could have snuck that screwdriver from Leroi's pickup truck." He paused, studying the grim faces staring at him. "Me, I look around here, and I see some who don't cry about A.D."

Another blast of wind struck, almost knocking us off our feet. "We're stuck here, folks. No one is going anywhere," I shouted above the pounding of the rain. "So we best make ready. We all need to pitch in and help put storm shutters up. Button the house up tight."

Walter Venable shouted to George Miller, "You and your family give us a hand, George. My folks'll bring out the shutters and you and yours start putting them up."

George wiped the rain from his angular face and grinned. "We'll put them up faster than you can get them out, Walter."

"Think so? Bet you a cold one. Leave a couple doors open for the time being. It gets real bad, we can fasten them down right fast."

Bailey headed for the house. "I'll haul some tools up from below. Hammers, nails, saws. Whatever we might need."

I grinned. "Good, now the rest of you. Back inside. Back inside." I helped Janice from the truck and we hurried up the steps.

Patric Thibodeaux tagged after Bailey. "I told you Leroi wasn't the killer. You blamed him because you never had any use for us anyway."

Remembering the bad blood between Patric and Bailey, I tried to stay close just in case their heated words exploded into action.

Bailey snorted. "Bull! Just leave me alone unless you want more trouble than you can handle."

Patric followed the larger man into the living room. "You know who killed A.D. It was John Roney. We all heard him threaten A.D. before they went upstairs to play poker."

With a sneer, Bailey shot back, "Maybe your boy didn't do it." He glared at Patric. "Then you tell me, how did John Roney get the screwdriver from Catfish Lube?"

"John Roney could have picked it up anywhere. Besides, he was in the room with A.D. when we found them. And there was blood on his hands."

I looked around for my old man. He was slumped on a vinyl couch, his head cocked back on the back of the couch, his mouth gaping open. Passed out. I held up my hands in an effort to gain everyone's attention. "Listen, folks. Listen a minute."

They paused.

"Let's all just take it easy. We aren't going anywhere. Let me try to contact the state police."

"Just how you going to do that?" Ozzy sneered.

All of our lives, Ozzy had tried to bully us because his pa was the rich one in the family. Even at forty-one, he still tried, and still without success. "Don't fret, Ozzy. I can do it." I studied the faces around me. "Don't get your hopes up, folks. They're not going to come out here until the storm passes."

From the back of the parlor, a voice called out. "Why can't they come out here in a boat?"

A chuckle of derisive laughter echoed through the room. George Miller replied. "Because there ain't no boat going to fight those four-foot waves out there."

As if to punctuate the remark, a blast of wind struck the house, rattling the windows and sending vibrations through every stick of wood in the mansion.

Chapter Four

The various branches of the family separated, seeking the security of closer kin. They gathered in the corners of the parlor, in the dining room, the kitchen, the living room, the library, and even at the top of the broad stairway leading to the second-floor landing.

For whatever reason, fortuity, fortune, or fate, my cell phone connected with its server. I contacted the Lafayette Police Department, and they passed word to the state police.

Fifteen minutes later, the Lafayette Police Department called back. I took the message, thanked them, and punched off.

"What did they say?" Bailey Thibodeaux asked.

"Like we said, they'll be out after the storm. They said to keep the scene pristine."

Uncle Bailey snorted. "What's pristine?"

I suppressed a grin. "Undisturbed, Uncle Bailey. They don't want us to move anything around."

A murmur ran through the crowd.

Bailey grunted and turned to his sister, Iolande. "What about A.D.? He's going to be stinking in a couple days."

The murmur grew louder. "We could bundle him up and put him out in the shed with the generator," Ozzy suggested.

Patric shook his head in disbelief. "That's the dumbest thing I ever heard, boy. Why, the animals, they'll have him carried off before morning."

"Then what do you suggest, Uncle Patric?" Sarcasm dripped from Ozzy's words.

Patric scratched his gray-shot hair and wrinkled his nose. "Hadn't thought on it, but maybe we could put him in the bathroom and seal the door."

Iolande snapped at him. "Don't be stupid. The smell, it stay in that room like skunk. Never it come out."

"Stick him out on the porch," Aunt Marie suggested.

"That ain't no better than the shed," Uncle Patric responded.

For the next five minutes, the family tossed suggestions around and argued among themselves. Men got nose to nose, pulling apart only to take a drink of beer or what moonshine they had managed to salvage.

When it appeared they might settle on wrapping A.D. in a sheet like a mummy and dangling him from a tree limb well above the ground, Leroi leaned over my shoulder and whispered. "We got to do something, Tony. I never cared for A.D. He cheated everyone in the family, but he's entitled to some respect. Even if he was no good," he added.

Janice nodded. "He's right, Tony. These people are scary. Do something."

I tried not to laugh at her consternation. Meeting an entire family of Cajuns in the middle of a family *fais do do* is quite a cultural shock for someone from her strata of society. For a refined and proper lady accustomed to daylily shows and country clubs, a visit to Whiskey Bend among the cypress knees and Spanish moss was like moving to another planet.

When the hubbub quieted, I said, "I'm not any kind of expert, and I'm not trying to be, but I have been around police and their procedures for the last few years. We can do some of their work for them. Maybe enough so when we move Uncle A.D., we won't destroy any pertinent information."

"Yeah?" It was Ozzy, his usual, sarcastic self. "What about Pa? What are you going to do with him?"

"Simple. After we take care of business up there, we'll place him in a sheet and put him in the freezer."

"But, he'll freeze up solid," Ozzy retorted, alarmed.

"Not for two or three days. Maybe the state police will be here by then."

"The freezer will be ruined," exclaimed Iolande.

"I'll buy another freezer," Janice quickly offered. "Gladly."

Bailey waddled forward and looked down at Janice as if she were some sort of curious specimen. "You that rich girl Tony goes with?"

Intimidated, Janice backed up a step and nodded briefly.

Bailey shrugged. "Fine with me."

"Hold on, Uncle Bailey," said Ozzy. "Let's hear what else Detective Tony has in mind."

I glared at my sneering cousin. I resisted the urge to pop him across the bridge of the nose. Maybe later. Maybe later.

"Yeah. What else you got in mind, Tony?" Patric took a step forward.

"All right. Normally at a police scene, nothing is moved until everything is measured, marked, and photographed. Now, I suggest that is what we do. Two or three of us can go up there and do the necessary work. Did anyone bring a camera?"

In one corner of the parlor, a Broussard held up her hand. "I did. A digital. I've got some extra disks."

"Fine. With the digital, I can send pictures to the police if they want them."

I expected some argument, especially from the Idiot, but he nodded in agreement along with the others. "All right," I said. "Who wants to go up to A.D.'s room with me?"

"I'm sure going," Ozzy said.

Leroi and Giselle stepped forward. "We'll go if you can use us."

For a moment, I stared at them. Something seemed different, and then I realized Giselle had changed tank tops. The first was red; this one was green.

I shrugged it off. With the humidity outside, our women changed into dry clothes several times a day at these shindigs. The men just sweated, tolerating the shirt plastered to their skin. "We need a tape measure and some chalk or something to outline the body for the photographs."

Pa was still on the couch, passed out. Even from where I stood, I could see the blood on the fingers of his left hand and on the soles of his shoes. That was the man we were going to take into our home? I didn't think so.

Outside, the wind increased, howling around the exposed eaves. Rain battered the storm shutters, rattling them in their frames. A square foot of shatter resistant glass had been set in the center of each shutter, providing a faint glow of outside light as well as permitting us to peer into the storm.

I looked outside. Although it was only late afternoon, the sky was dark as night.

I led the way to the third floor. Opening the door, I turned on the light. The smell of blood and stale whiskey enveloped me like a thick fog. In the middle of the room, A.D. lay on his side beside the poker table. Congealed blood had pooled about his head and shoulders.

A set of bloody footprints led to the door, then faded as they proceeded down the hall. "Pa's," I said, gesturing to the prints.

Ozzy started to push past me into the room, but I stopped him. "Not yet. Pictures first from this perspective."

"Huh?"

Giselle spoke up. "You heard him. Pictures first."

I snapped three or four from left to right, catching the

layout of the room. I repeated the procedure from the opposite side of the room.

Taking care not to step in the blood, I photographed the body from several angles, too absorbed in my job to pay attention to Ozzy. I should have realized how flaky he was, but I didn't.

"What do you want me to do with this?"

I turned to him and froze. He held the screwdriver in his hand. "What the—what do you think you're doing with that?"

He shrugged. "It's the murder weapon. I didn't want it to get lost. There might be fingerprints on it."

Behind me, Leroi muttered a soft curse. Giselle didn't mutter anything. She shouted. "Ozzy, you're too stupid to live."

He grew defensive. "What are you talking about?"

I shook my head wearily. "There are no fingerprints on it now, Ozzy."

He looked at the screwdriver, then frowned at me. "Why not?"

"Because, stupid," yelled Giselle. "You wiped them off with your own."

Slowly, it dawned on the Idiot just what he had done. He bit his lip. "Sorry, Tony."

But Giselle wasn't finished with him. "You should be, you dumb—"

I interrupted her. "Hold it. That's enough. It's done. We can't do anything about it. Let's just get on with the job at hand." I glared at Ozzy. "Put the screwdriver on the table and just stand over there next to the wall and don't do a thing unless I tell you. You hear?"

He nodded, still holding the screwdriver.

"Put the screwdriver on the table, I said."

Without a word, he did as I requested.

We measured and chalked, then photographed some more.

I glanced at Giselle. "Who found him?"

"I think it was one of the Venables. Walter's wife, Marie. She saw blood on John Roney's hand and shoes when he sat on the couch, so she went up to see where the blood had come from."

I frowned. Patric had said Pa was in the room when A.D. was discovered. Someone had his story wrong, either Giselle or Patric. "What time?"

"I don't know. Around three or four."

I studied the scene. "We saw A.D. downstairs about two, so that means that somewhere between two and four is when he was murdered."

Ozzy sneered. "Brilliant, Sherlock Holmes."

I shot him a hard glance, then pointed a finger at him. "I'm going to tell you something, idiot boy. You make one more sarcastic remark, and I'll throw you through that window, storm shutter and all. You'll have thirty feet to the ground to think things over."

He glared at me, but he kept his mouth closed.

I photographed the table on which the two played poker. I noticed smeared blood spatters on the cards and tabletop. On Pa's side, a couple of the cards were damp. Around the cards was the outline of a dried pool of liquid. I made sure to photograph them at an angle that reflected the dried liquid.

When I was satisfied we had gathered all the data we could, I spread a blanket on the floor and the four of us placed A.D. on it. We lifted the blanket onto another blanket, and carried the bundle into the hallway.

I went back into the room and took more photographs, this time without the corpse.

Back in the hall, I had Giselle go downstairs for more help. "He's a big man."

Half a dozen men came up the stairs. "Be easy," I said as they started down the stairs with the body.

The irony of that situation was that each of the six had been cheated by A.D., some more than once. I was surprised they didn't just simply roll him down the two flights of stairs.

The chest freezer had been emptied. It was against one wall in the pantry off the kitchen. The other three walls were lined with shelves filled with a variety of staples and canned goods. In one corner was a broom closet. The only entrance to the pantry was from the kitchen.

We turned A.D. on his side and gently lowered him into the freezer.

"Maybe we need to turn the temperature up some," Henry Broussard said. "We don't want him hard as a rock." He looked around at me. "Why don't you get on that computer of yours and get somebody to tell us what to do."

I shrugged. "I'll try. Right now, turn it to about thirty-two."

Bailey shook his head. "It's just low, medium, or high."

Leroi and I shrugged at each other. "Medium," I replied.

Back in the parlor, the families had split into camps, each camp having its own prime candidate as the murderer. Uncle Henry and his family gathered around the radio.

I decided to visit with each family, take whatever information they had, and then pass it along to the state police.

Just after I finished with George Miller and his family, Ezeline Thibodeaux, Bailey's wife, came down the stairs carrying a gold money clip with the diamond encrusted initials, A.D.T. She stopped in front of her husband. "Bailey, what were you doing with A.D.'s money clip in your suitcase?"

Chapter Five

A stunned silence fell over my family. The only sounds were the wind and rain battering the old house.

Belligerently, Bailey growled from where he sat next to my old man on the couch. "What are you talking about, woman?"

Ezeline frowned at his ill-tempered reply. She hesitated, then timidly extended her hand with the money clip. "This, Bailey. Isn't this A.D.'s?"

Bailey struggled to his feet as Patric pushed through the crowd and grabbed the clip from Ezeline. He stared at it, then stepped forward and gave Bailey a sharp shove. "You bet it's A.D.'s. How'd it end up in your suitcase, Cousin? And where's the money?" His tone was accusing. "You was so busy talking about lynching someone out there, maybe we oughta lynch you."

Bailey glanced around nervously. "I don't know what you're talking about. Last I saw that clip, A.D. was waving it under Tony's nose."

Patric arched an eyebrow. "Then how do you explain your wife, she find it in your suitcase?"

"I—I—ah. . . ." He shook his head. His eyes darted across the sea of faces, "I don't know."

Ozzy yanked the clip from Patric's hand and jammed it

in his pocket. "I can tell you what happened. Bailey's always hated Pa. He probably snuck a screwdriver from Leroi's truck. That would explain it. Then he decided to take the money clip." He snorted. "Search him and you'll probably find the money in his wallet."

Bailey snorted and jammed his hand in his hip pocket. "Here, look at my wallet, you little *secousse stupide*," he hissed. "It sure ain't got no money other than forty bucks we got to last us until Friday." He threw it at Ozzy.

Ozzy grabbed it in midair and yanked it open. His face darkened. He shoved the wallet back at Bailey. "You probably hid the money anyway."

With a growl, Bailey lunged for his nephew.

Leroi jumped in front of him. "Look, Bailey. Let's just all calm down. Try to—"

"You stay out of this," Ozzy shouted, taking a few steps back. "We don't need some black—"

Giselle spun Ozzy around. Her hand blurred, and the pop of her hand against his cheek cut through all the arguing. "You watch your mouth, Osmond Thibodeaux. You hear? We're all family here. All. You best not forget that."

Ozzy glared at her, his lips quivering. "Yeah, we're all family, most of us," he added viciously.

Giselle's cheeks colored, but she stood firm, her eyes fixed defiantly on his. Her hand rose halfway to her shoulder as if to slap him again, then dropped back to her side.

Ozzy looked away.

I held up my hands. "It's late. Everyone needs some rest. Maybe we'll see things in a different light in the morning."

Janice slipped her arm through mine. She was strangely silent. I felt sorry for her. Talk about culture shock. Straight from a ritzy daylily show in a swanky hotel to a crazy family in the middle of a hurricane in two easy lessons.

Ozzy stormed across the parlor to the liquor credenza beside the kitchen door. Giselle followed. "She sure is outspoken," Janice said.

"Always has been. Had to be. But she's a good person."

Ozzy picked up a bottle of Jim Beam Black Label from the collection of bottles on top of the credenza. Giselle opened a door and retrieved a glass from the rear of the cabinet. She handed it to Ozzy. They were too far away to be overheard, but after Giselle handed him the glass, she rose on her tiptoes and kissed him on the cheek. He responded by hugging her to him.

They spoke for a moment.

Janice squeezed my arm. "Looks like they made up."

"Yeah."

Leroi and Sally approached. "What now, Tony?"

"Beats me. Just hope everything stays quiet until the storm's over."

At that moment, Uncle Henry approached. "Bad news, folks," he said, glancing over his shoulder in the direction of the radio. "Belle is a Category Two storm now. They expect her to hit Category Three before morning."

I grimaced. Three. Up to a hundred-and-thirty miles an hour.

"Where's she going, Uncle Henry?" Ozzy had stepped forward, a bottle in one hand, empty glass in the other.

For a moment, Henry just stared at us. "Right now, they're guessing Marsh Island, maybe Morgan City."

I whistled.

Janice squeezed my arm. "Tony. What does that mean? Is it bad?"

"Depends," Leroi replied.

Sally gave her an unconvincing smile. "It could come straight for us, but chances are, it will veer east a bit."

Leroi shook his head. "Don't kid yourself. Too much water. Nothing in its path. If it goes in at Marsh Island, it'll come straight at us." He paused and added, "If it goes in anywhere between Marsh Island and Cameron, we'll catch the worst of it."

Janice looked up at me, her eyes filled with a mixture of alarm and fear. I grinned at her. "Look, it isn't all that bad. Category Two means winds of about ninety-five to a hundred-and-ten. All the trees around here will help break the wind. We're ten or twelve feet off the ground, so we shouldn't have any problem with the storm surge."

Leroi chuckled ruefully. "No, but the surge will play the dickens with our vehicles."

I cringed, thinking of my new Silverado. I'd only had it six months. It didn't even have eight thousand miles on it. Suddenly, an idea struck. "The bridge."

"Huh?" Leroi frowned at me.

"The bridge. It's eight or nine feet above the water."

Leroi's eyes lit up. "Yeah. The storm surge couldn't be that high."

"Surge?" With fear in her eyes, Janice looked from Leroi to me. "What do you mean, a storm surge?"

"Water. Rising water. As the hurricane approaches shore, it pushes a wall of water ahead of it. Small storms maybe push a foot or so."

Giselle came to stand beside Janice. "Not to worry," she said in an effort to reassure her. "It would take a monster storm to push twelve feet of water through here, so don't worry about that."

Janice looked back around at me. "Really?"

I hugged her to me. "Really." Mentally, I crossed my fingers. I looked at Giselle and nodded to Ozzy. "See you two made up."

She laughed and glanced at our cousin who was climbing the stairs. "He's going upstairs to drink himself to sleep all by his lonesome." She winked at Janice. "Oh, Ozzy's all right. Hot-headed and spoiled, but he's all right."

Leroi and I exchanged skeptical looks. "You bet," I replied. "Anyway, now, let's get the cars moving."

In less than an hour, we had all the cars and pickups parked on the bridge. Four-foot waves crashed beneath us. The howling wind grabbed at our clothes; the driving rain pounded us, stinging our flesh even beneath two or three layers of clothing.

Leroi and I stuck our heads together. He had to shout above the wind. "That's it. I hope it works."

"Me too," I yelled back, directing the beam of my flashlight back among the parked vehicles. "Is that everyone?" The rain looked like silver icicles in the bright light.

"Hold on. Here comes Giselle. Last as usual."

We laughed. When she reached us, I shouted above the roar of the storm. "Okay, let's get out of here." We lowered our shoulders into the wind.

By the time we got back to the house, family members were settling down. Only a few slept in one of the nine bedrooms upstairs. Most tossed mattresses and cushions on the floor, preferring the security of family nearby. Sleeping bodies lay everywhere, from library to parlor, from dining room to kitchen.

In the kitchen, we put Janice, Sally, and Giselle on the countertops. I sat at the table and booted up my laptop while Leroi filled the coffeepot with water. I laid my .38 out of the way on the cabinet, glad to be rid of its bulk.

Keeping my voice low, I whispered to Leroi. "We need to keep an eye out in here tonight."

He frowned at me. "Why? The storm?"

I glanced into the darkness in the rooms where the others were sleeping. "Not the storm as much as what it drives in here."

His eyes grew wide as he understood what I meant. "You mean snakes."

I chuckled. "Yeah, snakes and snails and puppy-dog tails. And whatever else tries to find a dry place. Once that water starts rising, the creatures head for high ground." I arched an eyebrow and pointed to the table. "And around Whiskey Bend, we're high ground."

Leroi scooted back from the table. "I got you. I'll get some of the others to give us a hand."

"Good idea. Just make sure all the openings are closed."

While he was gone, I checked the storm. As Uncle Henry had told us, it was a Category Two and heading this way.

I stared at the screen. Every ten minutes, it updated, showing the progress of the hurricane. I rubbed the back of my neck. I was tired, but not sleepy. I couldn't believe that only this morning, I'd left Austin. It seemed like a month ago.

I decided to begin putting together as much evidence I could collect and later send it, along with the digital attachments, to the Lafayette Police Department.

Currently, the obvious suspects were Bailey Thibodeaux because of the discovery of A.D.'s money clip in Bailey's suitcase; Leroi because he went upstairs before he left with me; and John Roney Boudreaux because he threatened A.D.

"Now," I mumbled to myself, studying the three names. "Why would any of them kill A.D.?" To me it was obvious—they all hated his guts—but if that were the definitive motive, then the entire family would be suspect.

Pa was playing poker with A.D. We all heard Pa threaten his cousin, but none of us took it for a legitimate threat. It was just the talk of a drunk.

Bailey, I wasn't sure. As far as I knew, he might be included in A.D.'s will. Even if he weren't, the money clip in his suitcase was a devastating indictment. I'd heard family talk all my life about how A.D. had cheated Bailey out of his inheritance, but I never paid much attention. Every family has its skeletons tucked away deep in a closet. Tomorrow, I'd get Mom and Grandma Ola aside for the real story.

I knew more about Leroi because he and I had grown up together.

When his mother, Lantana, married Patric, she took fifty prime acres into the union, her share of her deceased parents' legacy. She died in childbirth, and Patric turned into a drunk. During one of Patric's sprees, A.D. managed to swindle his cousin out of the land. Three months later, drillers hit oil on the property.

I shook my head and clicked on the digital pictures.

The screwdriver had penetrated the right side of A.D.'s

neck. Pa was right-handed. He could have very easily excused himself to go to the bathroom, then once behind A.D., killed him.

Why? There was no reason other than an argument. Had there been an argument, Pa, being drunk, wouldn't have bothered to make up some excuse so he could get behind A.D. No, he would have reacted instantly, and as emaciated as my pa was, he wouldn't have had the strength to lean across the table and drive the screwdriver through A.D.'s neck with his left hand.

I looked up as Leroi returned. "George and Walter said they'd help us keep an eye out for snakes and all."

"Good."

Outside, the wind howled. The rain fell in sheets. I rose and poured a cup of coffee.

Suddenly, a scream came from the center of the house.

Leroi bolted through the kitchen door. I dropped my cup and raced after him. We reached the parlor just in time to see Ozzy jerk the French doors open and stumble onto the veranda.

We both slid to a halt and stared at each other in confusion. "What is that idiot up to now?" I said in disbelief.

Ozzy staggered off the veranda into the darkness. "Grab a flashlight," Leroi shouted.

I hurried out into the storm. "Ozzy! What's wrong? Where are you going?"

He paused in the rectangle of parlor light spilling down the steps from the open door. He spun and stared up at me, his eyes wide with fear. He seemed to be frothing at the mouth, and he trembled all over. His face twisted in pain, and he grabbed his abdomen and bent double, at the same time staggering backward down the remainder of the steps.

By now, several family members had gathered on the veranda, stunned by Ozzy's bizarre behavior.

Without warning, he collapsed in convulsions on the rain-soaked ground.

Stunned, the rest of us simply stood in the driving rain

like dummies, watching Ozzy thrash about. Sally shoved us aside roughly. "Let me through."

A voice started to protest, but Leroi snapped. "Shut up. She's an RN."

"Won't do no good. It's a spell," muttered Uncle George.

Patric grunted. "Grow up, George. There ain't such things."

"Don't be too sure. There's things we don't know about."

Sally knelt in the water and mud beside Ozzy. His face was contorted by pain. Taking the flashlight from Leroi, she held Ozzy's eyelids open and shone the light into his eye. "Dilated. Convulsions." She checked his pulse and shook her head. By now, Ozzy was gasping for breath. Sally looked up at us. "Quick, get him back into the house."

Before we could respond to her order, a series of violent convulsions seized Ozzy, jerking him into a sitting position where he spewed vomit all over his lap.

He seemed to freeze in that position for several seconds, and then his entire body went rubbery, and he fell back to the ground.

The rain beat down on his face.

Ozzy was dead. Sally didn't have to say it. I knew. And to tell the truth, I was scared. We were caught between a killer storm outside and a lunatic inside.

We couldn't run because there was no place to run. Help couldn't come in.

Followed by a caravan of Thibodeauxs, Boudreauxs, Millers, Broussards, Melancons, and Venables, we carried Ozzy to the pantry and laid him on the floor beside the freezer. About the only adults missing were Pa and Bailey, both of whom I figured where sleeping off the whiskey and beer.

"Now what?" Uncle Henry Broussard looked at me.

I glanced at the freezer, but before I could reply, Giselle spoke up. "Oh, no, Tony. You're not going to put him in the freezer with A.D."

A scatter of murmurs came from the family.

Sally and Janice stood in one corner of the pantry. I could tell from the incredulous look in Janice's eyes that she could not believe the bizarre series of incidents of which she had become a part.

When she stepped out of her Miata convertible on the bridge earlier in the day, she left behind the familiar and comforting social climate of Austin, Texas, with its country club parties, bridge games, and fashion shows. She had stepped into a culture three hundred years behind hers. I smiled at her, but she didn't return my smile. She appeared dazed.

"Look," I said to Giselle. "I don't know what else to do. We're in the same boat with Ozzy as A.D. I don't know what happened to him, but—"

Sally spoke up. "A poison of some kind."

"What?"

Everyone turned to gape at her.

She nodded and took a step forward. "The symptoms point to it. Dilated pupils, convulsions, labored breathing, vomiting. Those together would in all probability indicate some kind of poison."

Patric frowned. "You ain't sure?"

Sally gave him a sad smile. "No."

Iolande, A.D. and Bailey's sister, said. "You're claiming one of us poisoned Osmond."

"No. I'm just saying the symptoms indicate poison. Only a toxicology test can tell us that."

George Miller grunted. "I bet a white nurse would know."

Uncle Henry Broussard spun around his weathered and wrinkled face twisted in anger. His eyes blazed, and he jabbed a bony finger in George's face. "Shut your mouth, George. You say anything like that again, and you'll be right down there on the floor with Ozzy. Leroi's wife, she knows what she's doing. We got enough problems here with one of our own trying to kill us all. We don't need any white trash talk. You hear me? You and that stupid voodoo nonsense."

Uncle George glared at Henry, flexing his fists. An eerie silence settled over the pantry. Tension rose. The only sounds were the winds howling around the eaves and the rain battering at the windows.

Uncle Henry took a step forward. "Now, you best hear me, George Miller. When we were kids, I could whup your tail, and I tell you now, *cher,* I can still do it."

George tried to outstare Uncle Henry, but his resolve wilted. He lowered his eyes. "All right. I didn't mean it that way. I. . . ." His words faded away.

I winked at Sally. She winked back.

We didn't know what else to do, so we laid Ozzy on top of his pa.

Chapter Six

The five of us climbed the stairs to Ozzy's room on the second floor, directly below his pa's. I don't know about the others, but I noted that no sleeping arrangements had been made in his room for others. He had planned on keeping the room all to himself. He was always selfish and greedy.

"You think it was some kind of poison, huh?" I spoke over my shoulder to Sally.

"That's how it looks."

A fifty-four-inch TV stood against one wall. Beside it was a cabinet of videos. A couch and two chairs were arranged in front of the French doors leading to the veranda. His king-sized bed stood against the third wall.

A half-full fifth of Jim Beam, Black Label, the bottle I saw him take from the liquor cabinet, sat on the nightstand. Next to the Jim Beam was a partially filled whiskey glass, and beside it was a plate with a ham sandwich from which three or four bites had been taken. An empty tumbler sat on the other nightstand.

Giselle reached for the whiskey glass. I stopped her. "Leave it here. Let the police take care of it."

She blushed. "Sorry. I wasn't thinking. I was going to take it and the plate down and wash them."

I grinned. "I know you probably keep a spotless house, Giselle, but this time, hold off on this room, okay?"

She laughed nervously. "Okay."

I took several shots of the room, first from one side and then the opposite, after which I photographed the nightstands. I turned to Sally and indicated the dishes on the nightstand. "This looks like the only place he could have picked up some poison. What do you think?"

She shook her head and slipped her arm through Leroi's. "You know better than me. All I know is that he displayed the symptoms of poisoning."

The dazed expression had faded from Janice's face. "Could there have been any other way for him to get the poison?"

Sally shook her head again. "An autopsy might pick up a scratch or bite."

Leroi looked at me. "Maybe it was a snake."

All of our eyes searched the room as one.

Sally said, "I don't know much about snakes, but I never heard of all those symptoms from a local species."

"I don't know," I replied, squinting into the dark corners. "Maybe we should take a look at Ozzy."

Giselle groaned. "Don't tell me you want to take Ozzy back out."

"No, we can probably look him over there in the freezer."

"Then we'd better get on with it," Leroi said. "Before he gets hard."

We all looked at each other. Despite the solemnity of the moment, a situation so bizarre, we had to laugh.

Giselle, Janice, and Sally sat at the kitchen table with me. Leroi leaned against the refrigerator. "At least we know he wasn't snakebit," he said.

"Which means that he probably ingested poison," Sally responded.

"Maybe it was some of Nanna's voodoo," Giselle said, a wicked grin on her face.

"Yeah," Leroi chimed in. "One of her *wangas*. That's what Uncle George claims."

I snorted and waved their sick humor aside. "In your dreams." I glanced toward the parlor, filled with the strangest feeling that Nanna was staring at me.

Growing somber once again, we sat there for the next several minutes, rehashing the night's events, talking over possible explanations, and coming up with nothing.

I leaned back in my chair and closed my eyes. I was exhausted, but despite my weariness, I couldn't shove aside the frustration eating at me. I felt as if I had no control over any facet of my life—not the storm, not the murders, not the fact my father was coming home to live with us. I had the hopeless feeling I was simply being dragged along behind an escalating chain of events bound for a catastrophic explosion.

I muttered.

Leroi glanced at me. "What's wrong?"

"Nothing." I shook my head.

"Sounded like something to me," Giselle replied, her tone edged with a trace of amusement.

I studied her a moment. "It's my old man," I blurted out. "He wants to move back to the farm with Mom and Grandma Ola."

Leroi's eyes widened in surprise. "You're kidding."

"Nope." I shook my head. "That's what Mom said."

Janice laid her hand on my arm. "How do you feel about it, Tony?"

"I think the idea stinks." And to my surprise, I realized that was exactly how I did feel. "He left us thirty-two years ago. He doesn't deserve to come back," I added, pouring out all the bitterness and bile that I had kept bottled up inside me for all those years.

Giselle leaned across the table. "But, he's your father. You only have one."

I cut my eyes toward her. "He only had one son, and he deserted him. Then when we did meet, he stole everything he could get his hands on." I shook my head emphatically. No way did I want him to come back home.

"Maybe, Tony," Sally said in a soft voice, "maybe he's coming home to die."

We all stared at her for a moment. That thought had never entered my mind. Still. "Well, maybe. I don't know. Let him find some other place," I replied. "I. . . ." I pushed back from the table. "Look. We all need some rest, even a few minutes. The sun will be up shortly. At least we'll be able to see outside."

Janice gave me a wan smile.

"Yeah." Leroi pushed away from the refrigerator and glanced at me. "You girls best sleep up on the countertop."

Giselle nodded to the floor. "What's wrong with a pallet on the floor? That would work. . . ." She hesitated, her eyes growing wide. "Oh, I see."

"See what?" Sally frowned at her.

With a crooked grin, Giselle replied. "Crawly things coming in out of the storm."

"Probably not," I said, not wanting to alarm them any more than necessary. "But, it couldn't hurt. Better safe than sorry," I added.

Leroi grinned crookedly. "The man's right, ladies. Like the old philosopher said, forewarned is forearmed. Or something like that. Tony, you take the table."

"What about you?"

He pointed to the pantry. With a wry laugh, he replied, "I'll sleep on the freezer. Be the first time in my life I can claim I came out on top of Ozzy and A.D."

We all laughed. Giselle shook her head. "Leroi, that's terrible, terrible."

His grin grew wider. "I know, but it sure feels good."

I lay on the table and stared at the ceiling. I tried to make some sense out of all that had happened. For a fact, one of our family had committed two murders, but who?

Unable to sleep, I rolled off the table and headed for the stairs. Maybe if I took another look at the rooms, something might click. As I ascended the stairs, I attempted to put together a logical theory.

A.D. had cheated many of those with whom he had dealt. I wasn't sure just which families had felt the sting of his chicanery, so I figured I would talk to them all.

I started with Uncle Bailey, born Bailey Claux Thibodeaux sixty-one years ago. Somehow, A.D. had shoved Iolande and Bailey aside and managed to get his hands on their parents' money and farm. I didn't know how, but I knew Mom and Grandma Ola could tell me.

There was no question in my mind that Bailey probably harbored resentment toward his brother who, along with his sister, Iolande, had lived in a half-million-dollar mansion on two thousand acres raising exotic animals while Bailey and his wife, Ezeline, eked out a threadbare existence in a shotgun shack in a rundown neighborhood in Eunice. He worked as produce manager in a locally owned supermarket.

I paused at the bottom of the stairs. A frown wrinkled my forehead. I didn't know what I would have done had I been in Bailey's shoes, but I knew myself well enough to know that I would never drink with a man who cheated me.

On the other hand, I reminded myself, Bailey might have simply sold A.D. his share of the estate.

And then there was Pa, who, I suppose, could have murdered his cousin. He had blood on him, but if the truth were known, he probably wasn't even aware of the blood. The damp cards on the table where Pa had been seated led me to believe that Pa probably passed out and drooled on them. He wasn't drinking beer, only whiskey. And trust me, you don't get condensation on a table from a bottle of whiskey.

He was probably unconscious when the killer murdered A.D. When he awakened, he staggered from the room, inadvertently brushing his hand in the blood spatters on the table and stepping in the pool on the floor. That would account for the smeared spatters and footprints on the floor.

And then there was Leroi. Guiltily, I glanced over my shoulder in the direction of the kitchen pantry.

He and I had gone to school together in Church Point. When I left for the University of Texas, he headed for Louisiana State, where he dropped out after two years. He worked, married, and opened his own lube shop, which by now had grown to four.

I suppose he could have held the resentment and desire for revenge for thirty-eight years, but I doubted it. Still, knowing that his uncle had swindled his father out of land Leroi's mother brought to the marriage was a motive not to be discounted.

And then there was the murder weapon, a screwdriver with a Catfish Lube logo on it.

The big question on my mind as I climbed the stairs was if the deaths were tied together, or whether Ozzy had simply ingested the poison on his own.

Why would he have done that? That was the question. On the other hand, why did he pick up the screwdriver? Was he deliberately trying to smudge the prints, or was he indeed trying to help, however clumsily? Perhaps he poisoned himself out of guilt for murdering his own father.

I paused outside Ozzy's room. Reluctantly, I opened the door and flipped on the light. A scurry of movement on the nightstand caught my attention. A dozen two-inch-long water roaches scrabbled off the partially eaten ham sandwich. I shivered. I hated cockroaches, noting with satisfaction that a couple of the prehistoric creatures had drowned in the half glass of Jim Beam. I studied the room once again, hoping for a flash of intuition, or perhaps even divine revelation.

Nothing.

The same in A.D.'s room.

Frustrated, I went back downstairs and climbed back up

on the kitchen table. With a sigh, I closed my eyes and thought back over my years with Blevins' Investigations back in Austin. I tried to remember all to which I had been exposed. I knew my limitations as a private investigator. I didn't possess the instincts of Al Grogan, the top sleuth in my boss's stable of P.I.'s back in Austin. I was becoming more perceptive. After five years, I had to be. But, I wasn't in Al's class.

One truth Al had taught me was that there is one unequivocal, indisputable, incontestable fact. Evidence does not lie. It cannot be intimidated. It does not forget. It doesn't get excited. It doesn't get bored. It simply sits and waits to be detected, preserved, evaluated, and explained.

Witnesses may lie, lawyers may lie, judges may lie, but not evidence. The last thought in my head as I drifted off into a restless slumber was that I had to gather enough evidence so that when it was interpreted, it would point to the killer.

And if nothing else, I thought, *I'll e-mail all the evidence to Al Grogan and sit back and wait for Austin's own Sherlock Holmes to provide me the answer.*

Slowly, I became aware of a hand on my shoulder, shaking me gently. Then a husky voice broke into my dreams. "Tony, Tony."

I jerked awake and stared up at Uncle Henry Broussard. The deeply furrowed wrinkles in his sun-browned face reflected his apprehension. Outside, the gray light of morning had replaced the darkness of night.

"What? What?"

In his lyrical Cajun dialect, he explained. "The radio in the parlor, I listen. The storm, Belle, she is moving to Category Three. She be coming ashore later this morning west of Marsh Island." He paused, his face grim.

I listened to the storm whistling around the house, rattling the windows, from time to time sending slight tremors through the house itself. "Marsh Island?"

He nodded.

"For sure?"

He nodded again.

I sat up. "That means it'll come straight this way." I did a few fast calculations in my head. From the coast to here would take about six or seven hours for the eye, and then about that long again for the last of the wind to pass. Twelve to fourteen hours longer, plus the surge.

Without warning, the lights flickered momentarily, grew brighter, then went out completely. Uncle Henry and I stared at each other in the dim light.

I looked in the direction of the generator shed. "The generator. Something's gone wrong with it."

Leroi stepped into the kitchen. "The freezer stopped. What happened to the lights?"

"The generator." I banged the heel of my hand against my forehead. "It must be out of gas. Why didn't I think of that? It's been running since yesterday afternoon."

I jumped from the table and hurried to the door. All the doors were shuttered and held in place with two-by-fours. I reached for one, but Uncle George stopped me. "It's too bad out there, Tony. The wind'll knock you off your feet."

"The generator is out of gas, Uncle George. That's why the lights went off. We've got to refuel it."

For a moment, he stared blankly at me. Then he nodded and opened the door.

The four of us, George, Henry, Leroi, and I stepped outside and caught the impact of the violent wind. It rocked us on our feet.

George leaned close to me. "We'll never make the generator shed in this wind and rain."

"We have to," I yelled.

Leroi shouted into the screaming wind, "Let's go under the house. Through the storage rooms. There's a door on the south side. It's closer to the shed. Find some flashlights."

* * *

Water was ankle deep in the dark storage rooms beneath the house. I remembered my alligator boots. For a moment, I hesitated, trying to shove the price of the boots from my mind. Either that, Tony, or go barefoot, I told myself. Some choice.

I clenched my teeth and stepped into the water. I kept the beam of my light on the water ahead of me as we waded toward the south door. I hoped my boots wouldn't encourage a family reunion of their own.

George's voice trembled when he spoke. "You—you think there's some snakes down here in all this water?"

I forced a laugh. "I doubt it. Probably all the alligators ate them."

Leroi groaned. "Thanks a lot, Tony."

Henry snapped, "You boys, you hush up. Pay attention."

The shelves were jammed with odds and ends, those useless items that you can't bear to throw away, but that you'll never again use. I paid them little attention. I was more concerned watching the water at my feet for snakes and hungry alligators.

From the south door, we squinted through the horizontal sheets of rain. The generator shed was barely visible.

Uncle Henry laid his hand on my shoulder. "Take this, Tony." He handed me the end of a cotton rope. "I find a spool of it on the shelf. You boys is stronger than me and George. We'll stay here and feed out the rope. You tie it off at the shed. That way, you don't get lost on the way back."

Leroi and I looked at each other. He nodded. "You noticed Uncle Henry didn't say we were smarter, only stronger."

I shrugged. "We're the ones going out there, aren't we? He must be right," I replied, remembering a hurricane when I was a teenager. The rain literally engulfed us. I couldn't see Grandpa's old pickup six feet away in the driveway. While this storm wasn't that bad yet, it would get that way, especially if the eye came through here.

I stuck the flashlight in my pocket.

Leroi wrapped the rope around his wrist several times and then we plunged into the storm, me leading the way, Leroi holding onto my belt.

I'd heard the old folks talk about the peculiar sounds generated by a great storm. They were right.

The wind wailed like a great beast in its death throes, piercing my ears with deafening shrieks. The howls came from every direction, punctuated by the sharp cracks of snapping limbs. It reminded me of the unearthly screams I had always imagined Grendel's mother made when Beowulf cut off her head with a sword forged by the gods.

The rain battered us from every direction, sending us stumbling and sliding to our knees, stinging our faces. Clinging to each other, we managed one step at a time until we reached the metal shed housing the generator.

The door was partially open, and when I threw it back, a five-foot alligator lunged at me.

My heart lurched into the heart-attack range. With a scream, I threw myself backward into Leroi, kicking out with my boot at the same time. "Alligator, alligator," I yelled, hitting the ground and rolling over and over, at each moment expecting to feel the gator's jaws close about my foot. I remember thinking that at least I wore my boots. I prayed his teeth couldn't penetrate the leather, even though I knew better.

I struggled to my feet and hastily looked about me. There was no sign of the reptile.

Now, a five-foot alligator isn't all that fearsome, not with about half of him being made up by tail, but when suddenly, without warning, four feet away, he's staring you in the face in the middle of a hurricane with his jaws agape, all you can think about is vacating the premises as fast as possible.

Suddenly, Leroi appeared out of the rain. I jumped and screamed again.

"Hey, it's me. Only me."

I closed my eyes and dropped my chin to my chest. "You scared the dickens out of me."

"What was that all about back there? What happened?"

He was standing only a couple inches from me. I shouted into the rain. "Alligator. You didn't see it?"

His eyes grew wide. He yelled. "Don't lie to me, Tony. I'm scared to death of alligators. This is no time for jokes."

Sweat mixed with the rain coursing down my face, stinging my eyes. The attack had shaken me. "Hey, I'm not kidding. When I opened that door, he was standing on his tiptoes ready to go."

Leroi looked around hastily. "Where he is then? You think he went back in the shed?"

Tentatively, I eased toward the open door, planning on keeping it between me and the interior of the shed. "We'll find out," I yelled above the howling of the wind.

Leroi grabbed my belt, hugging up against my back. I slapped his hand away. "Listen, if I start running, you better not be in my way."

"You don't worry about me," he shouted back. "You move one muscle, and I'm back up on the veranda."

At least we understood each other. I kept my eyes on the ground ahead of me. Best I could tell, all that lay before me was ankle-deep water.

I reached for the edge of the door and on tiptoe, peered around it, expecting to see the aggressive little alligator defending the shed. All I saw was water. "I don't see him."

"Be sure."

"How can I be sure?" I looked around at Leroi. "He isn't in the doorway, but he could have gone back inside." I had forgotten all about the flashlight in my pocket. The only explanation I had for forgetting was that when that alligator jumped at me, my short-term memory outran my feet to the door.

Leroi muttered.

"What did you say?"

"I said I sure wished I was back in Opelousas."

With a rueful grin, I replied, "I sure wish I was back in Opelousas too."

He laid his hand on my arm. "Let me up there. I got an idea."

He stepped around me and yanked on the rope. George and Henry played it out. Leroi rolled up several loops, then tossed them into the dark interior of the shed.

"What are you doing?" I shouted.

"Spooking him out."

"With a cotton rope?"

He looked around at me in disgust. "You got a better suggestion?"

I studied the situation a moment. With a shrug, I said, "Throw the rope."

He did. Three more times.

"Nothing happened," I shouted.

"I'll try again."

Six more times we tossed the loops back into the shed. Nothing.

"Maybe we're okay," I said into Leroi's ear.

He nodded, stepping around the door and easing forward. "I'll feel around the corner for a light switch."

"Be careful." I stayed right at his back. Then it dawned on me that the light switch would do no good since the generator wasn't running.

Before I could stop Leroi, he felt around the corner, running his hand up and down the wall. Suddenly, he screamed and jerked his hand back. "Snake, snake, snake!"

Chapter Seven

Leroi stumbled backward, slinging his arm, trying to dislodge the black water snake slithering down it.

Believe it or not, my cousin actually levitated.

Impossible? Well, there was no other explanation as to how one second he was in front of me, and half a second later he was ten feet away, and that tiny water snake was hanging in midair in front of my face.

I promptly levitated in the other direction.

The snake splashed down in the water and slithered into the storm, probably relieved to have escaped two idiots throwing ropes around.

Uncle Henry shouted from the house. "You boys all right?"

Leroi shook his head. "I'm not going in that shed."

I wasn't any too keen on the idea, but we had to supply fuel to the generator or else we'd be sitting in the dark. That's how I explained it to Leroi.

"Then, Cousin, me and mine will just be sitting in the dark. You couldn't pay me to go in that shed alone."

We were standing nose to nose there in the rain, our clothes clinging to our skin, my hair hanging down in my face. I pushed my hair from my eyes. I wiped the rain from my face and grinned. "At least you don't have to worry about getting hair in your eyes."

He glared at me, but he couldn't suppress the tiny grin struggling to tick up one side of his lips. "You play dirty pool, Tony. Okay. I'll go with you, but I won't go first."

That was good enough for me. I didn't tell Leroi, but I figured with two of us in there, if any snakes fell from the rafters, they had two objects to choose from, and they might just choose him instead of me.

We started forward, and I jerked to a halt.

"What?" Leroi said.

I reached in my pocket and pulled out the flashlight. "Would you look at this."

Leroi cursed. "You mean we had that all the time? Why you got to be the dumbest—"

"Hey, you saw me put it in my pocket. Why didn't you remember it?"

He opened his mouth, then clamped it shut. "Let's just get it done, okay?"

"Okay."

From the doorway, I shone the light into the shed. With relief, I saw the generator was on a four-foot-high slab of concrete with steps leading up to it. Eight cylindrical tanks of gasoline lined one wall, all tied into the generator by a common fuel line. Each tank had a cutoff valve.

Suspended from the rafters along the opposite wall was a pirogue. Garden implements, rakes, hoes, shovels, and cultivators, hung on a third wall.

Then we spotted the snakes.

Leroi groaned.

I shivered. "At least it's just snakes. You know they got bears and wolves out here in the swamp."

He arched an eyebrow. "And that's supposed to make me feel better?"

I shone the light around the shed. "Well, it isn't as bad as it looks. I count six snakes. And we're lucky. No cottonmouths among them."

His voice quivered. "Yeah, me too. I count six. I sure

wish Giselle was here. She's always had a way with animals. Now what do we do?"

I shone the light on the garden tools. "Simple," I said. "We'll grab a hoe and shove 'em out of the way."

"Okay, but what if they won't shove?"

"Then chop."

They shoved.

The generator had an electric start. Once it was primed with fresh gasoline, the engine roared to life. Lights flashed to life in the shed, and from the doorway, we could see the lights in the house.

Leroi and I grinned at each other. "We did it," I said.

"Yeah. But, before we leave, let's turn the other tanks on so we don't have to make another trip here."

The idea sounded good to me.

As an extra precaution, we tied one end of the rope to a metal stud in the shed. Once we reached the house, we'd tie off the other end, providing us a safety line to and from the generator shed if an emergency arose.

Outside, the storm intensified. Thick gray clouds raced from east to west, caught up in the massive circulation of the escalating storm. Treetops swayed almost to the ground. The slender trunks bent dangerously, and the thicker ones strained against giant roots, slowly wrenching them from the soft ground.

Back in the house, people were stirring.

Despite the storm, despite the two deaths, mothers prepared breakfast for their children, while the old men sat around and chewed on their situation in hushed tones.

Leroi and I slipped up to Ozzy's room and donned dry clothes. After drying my boots as best I could, I tugged them back on.

Back in the parlor, a single radio on a coffee table kept us all posted on the storm. Belle was moving, but slowly, just under ten miles per hour. Winds were almost one hundred, a Category Two.

I paused in the kitchen door, grateful she hadn't hit Three yet.

Mom was boiling up a large pot of coffee. I wanted to talk to her, not about Pa as much as the rest of the family, but the kitchen was too crowded. I figured if I had her alone, she would be less reluctant to fill me in on some of the old family skeletons.

"Coffee's almost ready," she said, brushing a strand of graying hair from her eyes and tucking it over her ear.

I nodded and glanced back into the parlor. Pa and Bailey sat on a couch in front of the shuttered French doors on the far wall, drinking beer and staring at nothing. I paused, my eyes fixed on them. Janice came up behind me. "Here, I have us some coffee."

Taking the coffee, I gave her a light kiss. "Thanks." The coffee was thick and hot, rich with chicory. "I can sure use this."

She took a dainty sip. Her eyes grew wide. She whistled. "This is strong."

I chuckled and took another drink.

She sat her cup on a nearby credenza and made an effort to smooth the wrinkles in her blouse. "Your mother always make it that strong?"

"Yeah." I grinned down at her. "In many of the old folks' homes, Cajun coffee and homemade bread is a treat for guests. Always been like that." I paused, then said, "I'll bet you didn't know what you were getting into when I picked you up on the bridge yesterday."

"Yesterday." She laughed and shook her head. "It seems like a year ago. But, it has been an interesting experience."

I arched an eyebrow. "Interesting experience?"

With a mischievous glint in her eyes and a determined jut to her jaw, she played down the seriousness of our situation. "One thing for certain, I won't run into something like this in the ballroom at Barton Springs Country Club."

Janice Coffman-Morrison might be rich, but she was also a tough and resilient woman, in the mold of her Aunt Beatrice Morrison, CEO of Chalk Hills Distillery and Janice's only living relative.

I hugged her to me. Not that she would marry me, but if I were the marrying kind, she was my choice. I'd been married once though. That too seemed a long time ago.

Diane and I were high school sweethearts, an affair that continued until she dropped out of the University of Texas and returned to Church Point. We ran into each other several years later, each still single. The next year, while I was still trying to teach America's brats, we married, but unlike most of our friends who made one baby after another because they believed it was their God-given mission to procreate the entire world all by themselves, Diane and I had no offspring.

Within two years, the thrill of lust and passion faded when we had to wake up each morning and face each other at our worst. We managed another couple years before we split the sheets.

The best thing I can say about Diane is we parted amicably. She took her clothes, the furniture, the car, and I took my clothes, a ten-gallon aquarium with my little Albino Tiger Barb, Oscar, his swimming mates, and a taxicab. Like the old country song from way back, "She Got the Gold Mine, and I Got the Shaft." But I never regretted the split at all. I was satisfied with Oscar and his cohorts, a few Tiger and Checker Barbs.

Once I put some angelfish in with the Barbs, but the little Barbs chased the docile little angels around the aquarium, nipping at their fins. The angels would probably have died of heart attacks if Jack Edney hadn't come along.

On a drunken spree, he urinated in the aquarium thinking—well, I don't know what he was thinking. Next morning, all except Oscar were floating belly-up. Oscar just swam in circles. Some kind of brain damage, I guessed.

Naturally, Jack, like all murderers, showed great remorse and regret when he sobered up, but the damage was done.

Janice took another sip of coffee and noticed I was watching Pa and Uncle Bailey. "How long has it been since you've seen your father?"

"Huh? Oh, a year or so. You remember. I told you about it." I stared at him, feeling nothing. Maybe I should have, but I couldn't give myself any reason I should have feelings for him. When I looked at that emaciated old man behind a week-old beard, so thin his clothes hung on him like a scarecrow, I couldn't believe he was a partner in giving me life. I shivered at the thought.

He bailed out on Mom and me when I was seven. I didn't see him again until last year when I found him stumbling about the streets of Austin. The first time I took him in, he stole my camera, what was left of a six-pack of beer, and the spare tire for my pickup. The second time, it was my sheepskin-lined coat, a VCR, and another camera.

Why should I have feelings for a father like that?

"You didn't know he was coming to the reunion, did you?"

"No. And now he wants to come back home."

Janice looked up at me. "You told me. I wonder why?"

"Beats me. It isn't to die like Sally said," I muttered bitterly. "But, I'll talk to Mom later this morning. See what all was said."

Uncle Henry approached. "George and me checked all the doors and windows. Shutters seem to be holding up." As if laughing at his announcement, a gust of wind rattled the shutters.

"There's your grandmother, Tony," Janice said, nodding to the broad stairs descending from the second floor.

Bailey's wife, Ezeline, was with Grandma Ola. I went to meet them. I gave Grandma a peck on the cheek and pointed both of them to the kitchen. "Mom's got coffee ready. See if you can talk her into baking some homemade bread."

Ezeline looked around. "Where's Iolande? She's usually the first one down."

Grandma Ola gave me a playful slap on the arm. "Go wake her, Tony. If we got to sit and worry about the storm, she does too."

Both old ladies laughed.

With Janice, I headed up the stairs, my boots squishing water. Giselle was coming down, brushing at a stain in her green tank top. "Hey," she called out with a bright smile. "Where you guys going?" She arched an eyebrow, her eyes glittering mischievously.

I pointed upstairs. "Grandma Ola wants us to wake Aunt Iolande."

Giselle grimaced. "She took A.D.'s death hard." She cut her eyes toward Sally and Leroi below in the parlor. Whispering, she added, "She swears Leroi did it."

"Because of the oil property?"

With a rueful grin, she nodded. "Yeah. You believe that?"

I glanced at Janice, then looked back at my cousin. "I can believe anything about this family right now."

Smoothing at the wrinkles in her own blouse, Janice turned to Giselle. "Oil property?"

"Yeah. Leroi's mother owned some land that A.D. swindled Leroi's pa out of after she died. Turned out there was oil on it. Iolande actually believes that Leroi has waited all these years to get at A.D." She quickly changed the subject. "By the way, I have some extra blouses if you want a fresh one. Might be a little large, but you're welcome."

Janice nodded. "Thanks. I might take you up on that."

Giselle looked up at me. "Who do you think killed A.D. and Ozzy?"

I half laughed, half snorted. "Hey, I don't know about Ozzy. I don't think Leroi killed A.D. I know he went upstairs before we left, but I just can't believe he did it. To tell the truth, at first I thought Ozzy might have."

Both women looked at me in surprise. "Ozzy!" they exclaimed simultaneously.

"His own father?" Giselle gaped at me. "You're kidding."

"Not at all."

Janice spoke up, "But, why?"

"Remember when we went into A.D.'s room yesterday? And remember how Ozzy pulled the screwdriver from his pa's neck? I figured it was deliberate, a surefire way of erasing any fingerprints while pleading ignorance." I shrugged. "Now, of course, he's dead. Kind of blows my neat little theory to pot."

Giselle shook her head. "I don't know, Tony. I don't think Ozzy was that clever."

"Maybe not, but it's a moot point now." I took Janice's arm. "Come on. Let's wake Aunt Iolande."

"I'll go with you," Giselle said, following after us.

Aunt Iolande didn't answer our knock.

Giselle giggled. "You don't think she's got a man in there, do you?"

I rolled my eyes. "If she does, she's had everyone fooled for sixty-five years." I opened the door slightly.

The overhead light was off, but the halogen lamp next to the wall was lit, casting a circular glow on the ceiling. I stuck my head inside, noticing a strong musky odor. I hesitated, trying to place the odor. Then I remembered, but quickly discounted the notion. It had to be something else, probably her perfume. I whispered to her. "Aunt Iolande. It's Tony. Time to get up. Grandma Ola sent me up."

She lay motionless under the sheets.

The rain beat against the storm doors on the veranda.

I called again, louder this time. Still no movement.

"She sure is a sound sleeper," whispered Janice.

"Well, I'll get her up." I grinned, pushed the door open, and flicked on the overhead light. I grabbed a corner of the sheet and popped it. "Up, or I'll yank it off." I popped it again, then gave it a yank.

In the next instant, a four-foot cottonmouth water moccasin lunged at me from the bed, his mouth wide open and his throat white as cotton.

Chapter Eight

Herpetologists will tell you that most snakes, even some of the poisonous species, are not aggressive unless you step directly on them. They will also hastily caution you that the cottonmouth is not one of that group.

Short-tempered and ill-mannered, he's in a class all by himself. Carrying a chip on his shoulder the size of a loblolly pine, he'll come after you just because he thinks the world belongs to him. And he won't waste any time.

Just as I didn't waste any time shouting at the top of my lungs and backpedaling, at the same time throwing out my arms to force Janice and Giselle backward.

Propelled by a fat black body with reddish-brown rings, the copper-burnished head shot toward me, its cottony mouth wide open and its curved fangs glittering in the light from the overhead fixture.

I shouted, "Back, back. Out of here! Cottonmouth!" I kicked a chair in front of the attacking water moccasin, at the same time cursing myself for leaving my .38 downstairs.

Janice stumbled backward into the hallway, but Giselle slid off to the left, along the wall. I grabbed the halogen floor lamp and jammed the lighted end at the oncoming serpent.

The heat and bright light caused the cottonmouth to pull up into a defensive coil. I was too busy keeping my eyes on the snake to pay attention to Giselle, but in the next moment, she pinned the cottonmouth's head to the floor with the head of a plastic broom.

Before I could say thanks, look out, or be careful, she grabbed the neck behind the head with her left hand and the tail with the right. She turned to the middle of the room and released the neck at the same time, whirling the snake over her head.

"Stay back," she yelled over her shoulder.

We stayed.

Like a whip, she whirled it twice more over her head, then with a sharp flick of her wrist, popped it at the wall. In the blink of an eye, the snake's head snapped off and struck the wall just below the family portrait of Iolande and her parents. Giselle tossed the headless body on the floor beside the twitching head. For a few moments the body spasmed.

"Don't get close to it."

That was one warning she did not need to give.

Both segments continued to writhe and squirm for a few moments. Then they ceased all movement.

Giselle stayed us with her hand. "Let me check first." She probed at the motionless shape with the broom. "All right. He's dead." She turned back to us and nodded to the blood on the floor. "Watch the mess. Probably some venom in there. Don't get it on your skin, especially an open sore or something." One side of her green blouse was speckled with body fluids from the cottonmouth.

I hurried to Iolande. The base of her neck and about half of her left shoulder were swollen and black from hemorrhage. In the middle of the swollen area around the carotid were two dark holes from which a bloody serum still oozed, running down her back. I laid my hand on her neck. She was dead, but her flesh still retained some heat. I guessed she had died within the last few hours.

We just stood there and stared down at her. Janice clutched my arm. Her voice trembled. "Tony, for heaven's sake, what's going here? Is someone trying to kill everybody?"

The question might as well have been rhetorical, for I had no answer. I laid my hand on hers. "I don't know what's going on. First A.D., then Ozzy, now Iolande." Without taking my eyes off the stiffening body of Aunt Iolande, I spoke to Giselle. "What do you think? Accident?"

She whistled softly. "I'm just a church secretary. I don't know anything about this sort of thing."

I looked at Janice.

The only sound was the wind and rain blasting against the house.

With Iolande's death, some of the family threw up a wall of denial. Too much had happened too fast to be true.

Giselle sighed deeply. "Poor Iolande." She shook her head. "So, now what?"

I frowned at her. "What do you mean?"

She nodded upstairs. "Iolande? What are we going to do about her?"

Before I could reply, I felt eyes on the back of my neck. I looked across the room.

Nanna stared at me, her pale fingers slowly massaging a velvet *wanga*.

On the other side of the parlor, Uncle Bailey had sobered enough to accuse Henry and George of not securing the house. He bellowed, "That snake had to come in some crack you missed." His words were slurred. Pa nodded, a blank look on his face.

"That ain't so," Henry said. "We checked everything—Patric, me, Walter, and George after the shutters was up. We poked sheets and towels under the doors, especially the two going downstairs to the storage rooms." He gestured toward Nanna. "That snake had to have already been in the house, unless you want to think some of that old woman's voodoo done it all."

Uncle George nodded somberly. "Them snakes, they do the work of the devil." He glanced at Nanna.

Patric snorted in disgust, his face almost black with anger. "It ain't no voodoo. Henry's right. We clogged up every hole. I'll take an oath on that." He glared at Bailey. Lifelong animosity bubbled to the surface. "Anyone says different will have to deal with me." He paused, then added, "At least nobody found A.D.'s money clip in my suitcase."

Bailey smashed his beer on the floor. "You got manure for brains. 'Course that don't surprise me none about some idiot that goes out and marries a nig—"

With a roar of rage, Patric leaped on Bailey, slamming the big man back on the couch and knocking it over, spilling Pa and them on the floor. Before we could pull Patric off, he got half a dozen punches in on Bailey who was squealing like a cut pig.

Patric struggled against us, but we managed to pull him off. "Nobody talks about my family like that," he sputtered at Bailey. "Nobody, cousin or not. You hear?"

We managed to get Bailey into the living room and Patric into the library.

After Patric calmed down, we went into the kitchen for some coffee. Sally and Giselle followed us. Giselle whistled. "I don't know about you guys, but I think I'd rather get out and face the storm than stay in here with all these nutcases."

I glanced uncomfortably at Leroi.

Giselle winced when she realized what she had said. A light blush touched her cheeks. "Sorry, Leroi."

He slipped his arm around his wife and hugged her to him. "Hey, I feel the same way."

I agreed.

Giselle glanced up at the third floor. "What about Iolande?"

Before I could reply, a voice called from the parlor. "Here's the next hurricane report."

We gathered around the radio. The eye was moving inland back west of us, the worse possible side.

Giselle muttered a soft oath. "I hope it takes a sharp cut back to the east."

Janice, who had never before experienced a hurricane, frowned. "Why? A storm is a storm, isn't it?"

Staring at the radio, Giselle shook her head. "Not hurricanes. They rotate counterclockwise. The strongest winds are on the east side of the eye. They come in off the Gulf with nothing to slow them down."

"Yeah," Leroi volunteered. "When the winds come ashore, they hit land, houses, trees, levees—all that helps break up the wind so that by the time it gets around to the west, it's lost about half of its strength."

I added my two cents. "If we're east of the eye, we catch the strong winds. If the eye goes east of us, that puts us on the west side where we don't catch nearly as much wind or storm surge."

Janice turned to Giselle. "That's why you want it to cut east."

Grimly, Giselle nodded. "Yeah."

Uncle Henry had been listening to us. He cleared his throat. "I figure we got six, maybe eight hours before the eye passes."

I nodded. That was what I had figured.

A ray of hope glimmered in Janice's eyes. "Then it's over, huh?"

"No." I shook my head. "It's half over. The wind switches from east to west."

Her shoulders sagged.

Before she had a chance to reply, a loud crack cut through the roar of the storm, and then the entire house shuddered as an ancient oak uprooted by the howling winds and torrential rains smashed down on the structure. Without warning, the sound of shattering glass and snapping wood sounded from the living room.

A foot-thick limb protruded through a window almost ten feet into the living room. Rain gushed through the hole. Uncle Henry's voice cut through the roar of the wind, "Poke blankets in the window."

Uncle George barked orders to his family, "Grab the axes and saws. Let's get this thing cut up."

Two children screamed, "Snake!"

Four snakes fell from a tangle of branches where they had taken refuge from the deadly storm.

Others took up the cry.

"Somebody kill 'em," shouted Henry, helping stuff the broken window with blankets.

Grabbing chairs and floor lamps, three or four of the young boys gleefully took up the chore of dispatching the snakes, completely oblivious to the fact they were smashing expensive furniture and hammering chunks out of the specially designed center-cut pine floor Uncle A.D. had paid a tidy sum to lay.

Uncle Henry yelped and jumped back from the broken window.

I jerked around. "What?"

His face had paled. He shook his head. "I ain't sure, but I'd swear I saw a bear out on the veranda." He eyed us sheepishly. "It was just a blur."

George Miller grunted. "Probably a bush or something the wind blew past."

Rolling my eyes, I grabbed one of the sheets and stuffed it in the broken window. "Whatever. Let's just close this up." A bear! Snakes first, now a bear. What next? The storm was getting to us.

After the limb was cut and the window covered as well as we could manage, Giselle cleared her throat. "Like I said before all of this started. What about Iolande?"

We were in the kitchen with Mom and Uncle Patric. I

threw up my hands. "I don't know. You all pitched a fit when I suggested putting Ozzy with A.D."

Janice eyed me warily. "What are you saying?"

I studied each of them. "Look, I have all the respect in the world for them, all three, even A.D. But I think we still have room in the freezer for Aunt Iolande."

Janice gasped. "Tony!"

Giselle shook her head. "Not Iolande."

I held up my hands. "Now hear me out. When they're autopsied, we want them to be as close to their physiological condition as they were when we discovered them. A.D., I don't figure, is as critical, but I'm guessing the venom in Aunt Iolande will continue to deteriorate the tissue. I don't know much about snakebites, but maybe if we can stop it now, there might be something left to help the forensic boys." I added, "And maybe there won't, but I say we have to give it a try. Same thing with Ozzy."

"I agree with Tony," Leroi said. "My only concern is if we have room in the . . . ah, the freezer?" His last two words faded to a whisper.

"I think so. Iolande isn't a large woman. Even if the lid won't close completely, we can drape some heavy blankets over it and turn the temperature colder." Even as we spoke, I couldn't believe we were having such a bizarre discussion.

For several seconds, no one said a word.

Sally broke the silence. "We aren't doing anything bad to them. I think it would be worse if we left them out for the natural deterioration process to continue."

Leroi eyed us sheepishly.

"What?" I demanded.

His grin widened. "Don't forget the smell."

Giselle gagged. Sally slapped his shoulder. "Leroi. That's horrible."

He held his hands out to his side in a gesture of helplessness. "Maybe so, but it's the truth. I'll never forget once when I saw them working on a body at the funeral home. He'd been dead a long time, and he sure smelled."

Giselle cleared her throat. "Maybe you're right. You think we should ask Bailey? He's her brother."

Janice looked up at me, questioning.

"She never married," I whispered. "Some say she was. . . ." I fluttered my hand.

Giselle interrupted. "Tony! Don't say such a thing about her. That's terrible."

"No," Patric replied. "Don't ask Bailey. You saw him. Drunker'n a skunk. Iolande, she was my cousin. I say we do like Tony, he say."

Fifteen minutes later, we had completed the task. The lid did not close completely, so we draped heavy blankets over the it and down the sides to help hold in the chill.

Mom had more coffee ready, so afterward, we sat around the kitchen table.

Over the last several hours, I had more or less laid out a plan of sorts for my investigation. To tell the truth, I felt awkward thinking of it as an investigation because it dealt with my family. On the other hand, there was a killer loose somewhere among the eight or nine families.

I told myself to approach this investigation just as I had the last few I had conducted. Forget it was family. Just ferret out the evidence, then let it speak for itself.

I chuckled to myself. It was easy to say, but a heck of a lot more difficult to carry out.

Bouncing around in my almost empty skull was a tentative list of suspects, but before I started really digging, I wanted to talk to Mom and Grandma Ola.

Alone.

Chapter Nine

Mom and Grandma Ola sat on a couch in the parlor. Grandma's dainty feet dangled just above the floor as she sipped coffee from a demitasse cup and nibbled on dry toast. She smiled up at me as I approached. "You always was a fine-looking young man, Tony," she said, the same praise every grandmother heaps on every grandson.

"Your genes, Grandma." I pulled out a small notebook from my shirt pocket. She eyed it skeptically. "Just notes," I said. "I don't remember too well anymore."

I learned early that detailed notes can often point out discrepancies when two or more people relate an event from their perspective or when they are asked to repeat the story.

She and Mom both laughed. "Your mother, she tell me you put Iolande with Ozzy and A.D."

"All we could do, Grandma."

"They trash. They belong together," she said sharply.

Mom gasped. "Mrs. Boudreaux. Don't say that."

Grandma shook her head. "Don't you act surprised, Leota. They family, but they the trashy kind." A good Catholic, Grandma Ola crossed herself. "I just hope they say plenty rosaries when they was alive. Nobody gots the money to say enough masses for them now they dead."

Mom laughed, and I joined in, but I noticed there was some restraint in her mirth.

"Was he the cheat everyone always said, Grandma? A.D. I mean."

She sipped from her small cup. Her eyes gazed into the past. "He all they say, *cher*. He be family, but he no good. A.D., he. . . ." She struggled for the right word in English. She snapped her fingers in frustration several times and looked to Mom for help. "*Un trompeur, filou.*"

"Mrs. Boudreaux. You don't mean that."

Grandma knit her brows. In a demanding voice, she repeated the words. "*Un trompeur, filou.*"

Mom shrugged. "Deceiver, swindler."

Grandma Ola nodded enthusiastically. "*Oui*. Deceiver, swindler."

I spoke to Mom. "So he really did cheat Bailey and Iolande like I heard. I mean out of their daddy's money. But if he did, why did Iolande live with him?"

Grandma Ola held up a knobby finger draped with translucent wrinkled skin covered with brown age spots. "That boy, he learn from his pa, Louis. Louis be your great-uncle. He my brother, but he was conniver. Your *grand-pere*, Moise, never do understand how Louis gots all his money. I know. Theophile, Patric's pa, he too dumb to figure for nothing. That's how come Louis gots the land Papa Garion left to Theophile." She sipped her coffee, tore off a small piece of toast with her fingers, and popped it in her mouth.

I paused in my note taking and raised an eyebrow to Mom. "Did you know all that?"

She shrugged. "I hear it. I never worry none. You do fine. Good education. Smart. The Lord has been good to us, so me, I don't worry none."

Clearing my throat, I laid my hand on Grandma Ola's. "Pa couldn't have killed A.D., could he?"

She didn't answer for several moments. When she did, she kept her eyes fixed on the broad stairs descending from the second floor. "The man I raise could not kill another man. This one here now, I don't know. He is not the child I brought into the world."

I looked from one to the other, noticing just how much my own mother favored Grandma Ola even though they were not blood kin. Glancing over my shoulder, I lowered my voice. "Who do you think did all this?"

Mom and Grandma exchanged looks.

Grandma Ola shrugged her rounded shoulders. "Me, I be ninety-one next birthday. The truth be that ain't no man who can't kill another. Some do, some don't. But all can."

I was getting nowhere, so I tried another angle. "You and Mom were on the veranda by the front doors yesterday when I got here. Now, sometime between two and four, A.D. was killed. I noticed the back stairs are still under construction, so the only way anyone could have gone up there and killed Uncle A.D. was by these stairs," I said, indicating the broad stairs sweeping up to the second floor. "Do you remember seeing anyone go upstairs?"

Mom frowned. "What time you say, Tony?"

"Two to four. Beginning just after I saw you and ending when all the commotion started after they found A.D."

Mom frowned. "That's hard to remember, Tony."

I squeezed her hand. "Try."

"They was A.D. and John Roney, for sure," said Grandma Ola.

"I saw Leroi. And—ah, I think Ezeline, Bailey's wife," Mom said.

Grandma Ola nodded emphatically. "*Oui.* Ezeline, and Marie, Walter's wife. She go up with Ezeline."

Mom looked at Grandma. "Don't forget Bailey and Iolande. They go up."

"Slow down. I can't write that fast." I was beginning to wonder if everyone in the whole family hadn't climbed the stairs. "What about Uncle Henry or Patric?"

Grandma mulled the question, then shook her head. "No. Osmond. I see Osmond, and they was a bunch of children running up and down, but, I don't remember Henry or Patric."

"What about Giselle or Sally?"

Mom and Grandma studied each other, then shook their heads. "Never see Sally. Giselle, she go in kitchen after you and Leroi leave," Mom replied.

"But not up the stairs."

She shook her head. "No."

Grandma Ola looked up at Mom. "That be all I remember. You think of someone else, *cher?*"

Mom frowned, concentrating. "Marie. Did we say Marie?"

Grandma Ola snorted. "*Oui.* I say Marie. She go up with Ezeline."

"Oh. Then, that must be all."

Tucking my notebook back in my pocket, I glanced around the parlor, wondering who else I could ask about the stairway.

Nanna sat in a wicker chair in the corner, her eyes closed, her jaws working, her lips moving, her bony fingers stirring an assortment of stones, dirt, bones, and straw, ingredients of her *gris-gris.*

I never gave any credence to voodoo or *gris-gris*, even though Nanna, my great-aunt once removed, practiced it. Of course, when I was growing up, every law officer in our town carried a *gris-gris* for protection, and on more than one occasion I'd heard family members ask Nanna to make a *gris-gris* for fortune or a *wanga* to place a hex on another individual.

But, as far as I was concerned, it was foolishness. No, Nanna would not be of any help to me.

But then I remembered the phrase Nanna had uttered the day before. I studied the old woman, her leathery skin wrinkled as a French accordion. I began to wonder if there might be something more to that voodoo business than I thought. Without taking my eyes off her, I asked Grandma

Ola and Mom. "What does *Ils sont dechire ce soir* mean? Nanna said it yesterday."

Grandma Ola frowned up at me. "Nanna, she say that?"

I nodded. "Yes, ma'am."

She pursed her lips and looked up at Mom. "The old woman, maybe she do see."

I looked around. "What do you mean, 'she do see'?"

With a shrug, she replied. "She say 'they be tears tonight.' "

I had the feeling I'd missed something. "So?"

Grandma Ola shook her head wearily. "Sometime, Tony, you be dumb as the next Boudreaux man."

"Okay. So what does it mean?"

"It mean, she see what done happened before it happened."

I studied Grandma Ola. There was no amused glitter in her eyes, nor faint smile on her lips. "You're serious, aren't you?"

She nodded. "*Oui.*"

I spotted Marie Venable and her family around a coffee table in another corner of the room. I headed her way, but Nanna stopped me, her eyes still closed. "You, boy. You be Ola's grandson." It wasn't a question. It was a statement of fact.

"Yes, ma'ma. Tony. Tony Boudreaux. You remember me?"

Brown spittle gathered at the edge of her lips. She snorted. " 'Course I 'member. Me, I don't forget no one."

For a moment, I studied her. Then I decided to see if Grandma was right. "What did you mean yesterday when you said *Ils sont dechire ce soir?*"

She looked up at me through filmy blue eyes. "Me, I mean what I say. They be tears tonight. Why you ask?"

"How'd you know what was going to happen?"

Her thin bony fingers rubbed lightly over a velvet *gris-gris*. "I know," she replied simply.

I nodded and started backing away, figuring I could learn nothing from her and anxious to see what I could find out from Marie Venable. "That's good. I'll talk to you later. Right now—"

Her eyes drifted shut, and she froze, her fingers stiff and motionless in the tiny piles of detritus on the table before her. Slowly, she opened her eyes and looked up at me. She extended her arm, her fingers offering me a tiny red velvet bag of *gris-gris,* protection for me. For a moment, I considered rejecting the bag, but I couldn't see any sense in hurting the senile old woman's feelings. I took the bag as she said, "You not find what you want. You find what you do not want."

I frowned at her. *Loony old woman,* I told myself. She was talking in circles. But then, what could you expect from someone well over a hundred—maybe closer to a hundred-ten? I brushed her off. "Yes, ma'am. I understand. Thanks." But I didn't understand.

Not that I could have done anything about it.

What had happened, had happened. The wheels of fate had been set in motion. I didn't know it at the time, but I had as much of a chance to stop it as I had of stopping that hurricane bearing down on us.

I slipped the *gris-gris* in my pocket.

Marie Venable nodded emphatically. "Yes, I go up to Ezeline's room with her. She had a new blouse she got on sale at Carpenter's in Eunice." She spent the next couple minutes describing the blouse.

"Did you see anyone else upstairs besides you and Aunt Ezeline?"

She pondered the question. "Well, Leroi, he was coming down when we were going up. When I come down, Osmond, he go up." She shook her head. "Maybe some more, but them, they are the only ones I know for sure." She paused, then asked, "Do you know who do all those terrible things?"

"No." I held up my pen. "All I'm trying to do is gather what information I can while it's fresh on our minds. I'll pass it on to the Lafayette Police or state police. I heard that you discovered A.D."

Her face blanched. She nodded imperceptibly. "I see your pa on couch. He got blood on his shoe and hand. I go up and find A.D. on floor."

"Then you came back downstairs."

Before she could reply, the sound of breaking glass and frantic shouts came from the second floor.

Half a dozen of us raced up the stairs. Leroi was right on my heels, and I was only a step behind Patric and George. They turned down the hall and slid to a halt.

Ezeline was standing in the hall, swinging at a black object protruding through a shuttered window. I blinked, unable to believe my eyes.

The rotund woman was screaming, flailing away with a walking cane at the paw of a bear.

"What is that?" Patric shouted.

I grabbed a chair and smashed it over the paw. The bear jerked back, then slammed the paw through the shutters and windows again. "What does it look like? A bear! The bear Uncle Henry saw." I shoved Aunt Ezeline toward the stairs. "Over there. Out of the way."

She stumbled backwards.

Bailey shouted, "I'll grab a gun." He spun and headed for the third floor while we hit at the paw.

Outside, the snarls and growls of the black bear roared above the clamor of the storm. He smashed at the window again. We pounded his paw with our frail weapons.

Ezeline stumbled forward. The bear lashed out at her, but Giselle yanked the frightened woman from harm's way.

Abruptly, the paw vanished. The growls ceased.

"Where'd he go?" Giselle called out.

"He's gone," someone shouted.

I turned to Giselle. "Am I glad to see you. Where'd you come from?"

She pointed to the stairs. "The stairs. With Uncle Henry."

Uncle Henry shouted from the corner at the top of the stairs, "What's going on?"

Patric jabbed his hand toward the window. "Bear! A bear! Someone look out there. See where he is."

"Not on your life," exclaimed Leroi. "About the time I stick my head out there, he'll stick his in."

Without warning, glass exploded from another window down the hall. From the stairway, Bailey shouted. "Here I come. Everybody stand back."

He slid to a halt in front of the broken window and emptied the clip. The paw vanished, followed by a roar of pain.

Quickly, we stuffed blankets in the broken windows. "It'll have to do until the eye of the storm gets here," I said.

The others nodded, realizing what I meant, dreading the idea of going out to repair the damage.

"We won't have long to fix it," Uncle George said.

As if in response to his remark, another storm shutter down the hall started banging against the window frame, ripped loose from its lock by the violent wind.

"Well, then," Bailey answered, looking in the direction of the loose shutter. "We'll just have to do the best we can."

Chapter Ten

Before going back downstairs, we decided someone needed to be on watch just in case the bear should pay us a return visit. Usually, black bears weren't aggressive, but given his circumstances, I couldn't blame him. All he wanted was a refuge from the storm.

We set up a rotating schedule.

"There could be more," Uncle Henry suggested.

Janice frowned. "More? You mean bears? I didn't think there were any bears around here."

Leroi shook his head. "Still a lot of black bears, and some panthers. They all retreated to the swamps as cities grew up. These storms push them to higher ground."

Shivering, Janice looked up at me. I slipped my arm around her shoulders. "Can't blame them. I'm surprised he came here. Usually, they just shimmy up a tree and curl up in a fork high above the water."

She cast a worried look at the windows. I chuckled. "Don't worry. They can't get in."

Uncle George volunteered to take the first watch.

"All the windows and doors are shuttered," Patric said. "He'll have to break through, so you'll be able to hear him."

"I'll hear him," Uncle George said. "I just had an idea.

Why don't some of you take down three or four doors on each floor. Dig up some hammers and nails and use them to nail over these broken windows up here. That'll work better than sheets. When we get a chance, we can get outside and nail the shutters down."

We nodded to each other. It was a good idea.

I started on the third floor. Janice, Leroi, and Sally pitched in. We removed the two doors beyond Iolande's room. I paused outside her door, shaking my head at her horrible fate.

Cursing the cottonmouth, I opened the door and peered inside for another look at the deadly creature.

I blinked. My eyes grew wide. Janice looked around my shoulder. "What's wrong?"

Incredulous, I stammered, "The—the cottonmouth. It's gone. It isn't here." Flipping on the light, I hurried across the room.

Janice clutched my arm and gasped. "Tony! Where did it go?"

"You sure it was dead?" Leroi stopped beside us.

My head spun in disbelief. "It's head was popped off. It bounced off the wall just below that picture."

"You sure? I don't see any blood," Sally said, looking around the room.

"There's got to be," I exclaimed, inspecting the wallpaper and the floor. But she was right. There was no trace of blood on the wall, none on the floor. I looked around. "Janice can tell you. Giselle popped the snake's head off and threw the body down here." I pointed to the floor at my feet.

Janice caught her breath and pressed her hand to her mouth.

Leroi blew softly through his lips. "Then where is it? What happened to it?"

I stared at the spotless floor. "I don't know. For the life of me, I don't know."

* * *

Half a dozen theories surfaced after we told the family about the missing cottonmouth, theories as bizarre as the two parts growing back together or a second snake swallowing the dead one.

"The killer took the snake," Patric proclaimed. "That's the only explanation."

Uncle Henry spoke up. "They said all the blood had been cleaned up. Why would the killer do that? Huh? What he trying to hide?"

Patric had no answer. None of us did.

Uncle George crossed his chest and glanced heavenward. He shook his head. His angular face resembled a sad horse. "You know as well as me. I say it once. There be things that happen that got no explanation. They be devil's work."

Bailey snorted. "Don't start up with none of that voodoo nonsense, George."

George looked around at his cousin. "Then you tell me where the snake, it be gone." He jabbed a bony finger toward the larger man. "I tell you this, Bailey Thibodeaux. There be things you and me don't understand in this world. Like it or not."

Bailey did not respond. For a moment, the same thought ran through all our minds.

Giselle broke the silence. "All I know is that I killed that cottonmouth. I popped his head clean off."

Nanna's words from the day before rang in my ears. "*Ils sont dechire ce soir.*" Could those words truly have been a precognition of A.D.'s death? Grandma Ola believed so. If that were the case, then believing the cottonmouth was phantasm voodoo was a small, though incredible, step.

Later I sat in the kitchen with Uncle Patric. "Ah," he sighed, sniffing the rich aroma of Mom's coffee. "That I need," he said.

I poured us two cups, brimful. The others had remained in the parlor. Placing my cup on the table, I leaned forward, resting my elbows on the table. "I want to talk to you about all this, Uncle Patric. Okay?" I pulled out my notebook.

"The snake again?"

"No. The murders."

A spark of irritation flashed in his black eyes, then vanished. He pursed his lips and wrinkled his button nose. "I tell you now, me, I don't believe in none of that voodoo even though Nanna, they say she sees things. But, we all family here, Tony. Even Bailey, though he don't act like it."

It was impossible to push the missing cottonmouth out of my mind, but I made the effort. "I know. But you and I both know someone in the family is responsible for your cousins and Ozzy. I've got no idea who it could be. As far as I know, the killer might be looking at you next."

He arched an eyebrow. "Or you."

I studied him a moment, wondering, then I nodded. "Or me."

Uncle Patric was short and thin, his curly black hair showing traces of gray. "But, you right. What do you want to know?"

"First, you told me yesterday that Pa was in the room when they found A.D." I checked my notebook. "In fact, you said 'when we found them.' " I looked up from my notes. "Did you find them?"

He ran his short fingers through his hair. "*L'oh mon non.* Oh, my no. Me, I not find them." He shrugged and sheepishly added, "I hear what others, they say."

"So, you don't know if Pa was there when they found A.D. or not?"

He knit his eyebrows. "Your pa, he was playing poker with A.D. when it happen."

I grinned at him. "I know. Who told you about the murder?"

"Ezeline. Maybe she find them."

"All right, Ezeline. Now, here's what I know so far. Ezeline, Marie, Pa, A.D., Bailey, Iolande, and Leroi went upstairs. Those are the ones I want to talk about first."

Patric waved his hand back and forth. "Not Leroi. He never do nothing like that."

"I don't think so either. But he was seen going up the stairs, and the murder weapon was one of his screwdrivers. All I want you to do is answer a few questions for me. I figure if we jot down this information while it is fresh on our minds, then that should help the state police when they get here."

He studied me a moment, then sipped his coffee. "What you want?"

"Iolande first. What do you think the chances are that she stabbed A.D. and poisoned Ozzy, and then accidentally climbed into bed with a cottonmouth?"

Uncle Patric snorted. "Not much, Tony."

I nodded. "Me neither. So that leaves Ezeline, Marie, Pa, Bailey, and Leroi."

"Of that group, who would have reason to kill A.D.?"

His face darkened. "I say not Leroi."

"I know, but the others. Which of the others would have reason to kill A.D.?"

A smirk smeared a sneer across his lips. "Most all. My cousin, he steal from whole family," he said, making a sweeping gesture that took in the entire kitchen.

He punched himself in the chest. "Me. He steal from me. He steal from my papa. I once think about shooting A.D." His voice dropped lower. "Once, when he drive down the road in his fancy Cadillac, I put crosshairs of my deer rifle on his head. I think then to kill him." He laid a single finger on the image of St. Peter, patron saint of fisherman, which dangled from the silver necklace around his neck. "But, I do not. I know from the priests that one day my cousin will answer for what he do."

"What about the others?"

He shook his head. "Your pa, he big drunk. He don't have the muscle. My boy—no." His shoulders slumped.

His voice grew soft, filled with remorse. "I give my boy nothing, only a life others joke about. He make something of himself. Not because of me, but because he be a good man." He paused to sip his coffee. "Iolande? She got no reason. She and A.D., they like that," he said, holding up crossed fingers. "Of all you mention, Ezeline, she be the one with most hate in her heart."

I sat back, stunned. "Ezeline?"

A faint grin played over his wrinkled face. "That surprise you, Tony?"

I forced a nervous laugh. "In a word, yes."

"Ezeline, she never forgive Bailey for letting A.D. cheat him out of the family money. She hate A.D. for what he do. Ezeline, she don't like living in a shack while A.D., he live in big house in country. The only reason Bailey come to reunion is because Ezeline insist. She say A.D. owe them something for what he done stole."

I considered Patric's answer. Looking at the story the way he told it, a couple pieces of the puzzle fit together. She could have gone into the room, found Pa passed out, killed A.D., stole his money clip, and later claimed she found it in Bailey's suitcase.

But why would she deliberately put the blame on her husband? Was their life so miserable? On the other hand, Ezeline could be desperate. She had no job skills. She had never worked. If Bailey were included in A.D.'s will, and ended up in prison, all the money would be Ezeline's. Not a bad motive.

For every question answered, I found half a dozen more without answers.

"Was Bailey in A.D.'s will?"

With a shrug, Patric shook his head. "I don't think so. After A.D.'s wife die, I figure he leave everything to his children, Osmond and Bonni." He paused, then added, "Maybe Iolande in the will."

I studied the coffee cup in my hands. "Even so, now it's

just Bonni. She'd be the perfect suspect if she were here. Where is she? You know?"

"*L'oh mon non.* She go two, maybe three years back. A.D., he spend much, but she not wants to be found, so he don't find her."

"What about Marie? She's the only one left who had gone upstairs."

"No. Marie's husband, Walter, he smart enough that A.D., he don't cheat him much. The first time, he do, but afterward, Walter know what to do. They not rich, but they got enough to keep gumbo in the pot."

I nodded, studying my notes.

Patric's voice dropped to a whisper. "There be one I not blame if she kill A.D. and Iolande."

"Huh?" I looked up sharply. "But who? We've talked about everyone that went upstairs."

He nodded. "*Oui.* She not go upstairs, but if she know the truth, then she have more reason to hate A.D. than anyone."

I was puzzled. "Who?"

Uncle Patric nodded to the parlor. "Giselle."

"Giselle?" I stared at him in disbelief, my jaw dropping open.

He leaned forward. "One reason be A.D. her father. But she don't know. No one ever tell her. Not her mama, Affina, not A.D. her papa. Me, I think maybe only them two, they know."

I'm not too swift to begin with, but when someone yanks that kind of family skeleton from the closet, it can blow a few brain cells. "But—but Affina and A.D., they're cousins. Affina and A.D. are cousins."

Patric arched his eyebrows and shrugged. "*Oui.*"

I eyed him skeptically. "How do you know all this?"

He shrugged. "Once, when A.D. drink too much, he gots all teary-eyed and told me. He don't remember nothing later."

For several seconds, I stared at him, trying to fit his stunning revelations into my own sense of order and propriety.

They didn't fit.

"I still can't believe it. They're cousins."

Patric smiled sadly. "And my boy is black."

I leaned back and stared blankly at my uncle. Now I understood why he stayed drunk so much.

A thought popped into my head. "You said 'one reason was that A.D. was her father.' Is there another? Is there something else?"

Uncle Patric glanced surreptitiously around the parlor. "A.D. and Iolande, they send Bonni away. She fool them and don't go where they say. Now they don't know where she be."

He had me confused. "What does that have to do with Giselle?"

"Giselle, she good woman. Help family always. Me, I think fine woman, and I always feel sorry because she never have no one close to her." His voice dropped to a whisper. "I don't know what you hear, Tony, but Giselle, she is different. Her and Bonni . . . they go much places together . . . they are very close to each other . . . more than family kin." He grimaced, trying to decide how to say what he wanted to say. "A.D. and Iolande, they don't want Bonni spend so much time with Giselle, so they send her away." He shrugged. "Me, I don't know if Giselle, she knows why Bonni leave or not. Me, I'm just an old man who don't know much." He hesitated, a slight grin playing over his lips in relief of having said what he did.

"What did it hurt how much time they spent together?"

Patric cleared his throat and stared at the ceiling. "Not so much the time together, I don't think. They just think Bonni, she should have friends more her age than Giselle. They think Bonni, she should find her a nice young Cajun boy."

Naïve me, I still didn't understand exactly what he was

trying to tell me. Like two blind men playing catch, Uncle Patric would toss out an implication, and I'd miss it.

Before I could pursue the matter, Leroi came into the kitchen. He shook his head. "The storm stalled. She isn't moving."

I closed my eyes and dropped my chin to my chest. I shoved Patric's information back into the recesses of my brain and muttered a soft oath at the latest change in the storm. Outside, the wind and rain blasted the house. I couldn't help wondering how the families down in the village were managing. Their shelter was cedar and cypress clapboard, not brick like ours.

My mind wandered back to Giselle. Everyone in our family knew she was illegitimate. It had been one of the whispered secrets cussed and discussed at every family gathering. Everyone knew, but no one admitted it. But, now—if what Uncle Patric said was true—why, that was—I couldn't say the word.

Leroi stuck his head in the door. "Any coffee there?"

Patric waved him in. "Come here, boy. Me, I gots a question."

Leroi frowned at me and shrugged as he came up to the kitchen table. "Shoot."

"Yesterday, you say you come inside to use the john. You go upstairs. Why you not use the toilet down here?"

It was a good question, one I should have asked, but like I said, I'm no Al Grogan.

Leroi sighed wearily. "Someone was in there, Pa. I didn't want to waste any time because Tony was waiting out in the truck for me so I went upstairs. Okay?"

Patric glanced at me, a smug grin on his face as if to say, "You see. It wasn't my boy."

I winked at Leroi. "That's what I figured, but how do you explain the screwdriver?" I looked from one to the other.

Patric shrugged. "That easy. Anyone could open the toolbox in back of Leroi's truck. Anyone."

That's how I figured it also. I just wanted one of them to say so.

The lights flickered once, twice, then continued burning steadily. Patric cleared his throat. "The generator? We got enough gasoline?"

"Sure, Pa. There's several tanks in the shed. Looks like they ought to hold about two or three hundred gallons each."

Giselle and Janice came into the kitchen. Janice poured some coffee while Giselle updated us on the storm. "Started moving again, heading back east."

I grinned at Janice as she plopped down in the chair next to me.

"That's good," I replied, making an effort to be jovial. "Means we'll be on the best side of the storm."

Leroi snorted. "If there is a best side."

Giselle laughed. "Always the pessimist."

Setting her coffee down, Janice ran her slender fingers through her short, brown hair. Pinching the midriff of her wrinkled and stained blouse between her fingers and thumbs, she pulled it out and fluttered it up and down. "If the offer still goes, Giselle, I'll take you up on one of those blouses. I've had this one on so long, it's beginning to feel like another layer of dried skin."

"Sure." Giselle pushed back from the table. "Let's go up and get you one."

"Think I'll listen to the radio a spell," said Patric, rising and following the girls from the kitchen.

Leroi and I sat alone in the kitchen, listening to the howling wind scream around the eaves. He glanced at me. His voice was a mere whisper. "Tony, about that snake. You don't think Uncle George was right, do you?"

I studied him a moment, my own thoughts still confused. "No. I don't know what happened to the snake, but it wasn't voodoo." I shook my head, deliberately ignoring Grandma Ola's beliefs. "That just doesn't happen."

He nodded. "That's what I thought. But, still, it's weird.

I mean, the way it vanished and the place was cleaned up. Makes no sense," he continued, rising and leaning over the kitchen sink so he could peer through the glass insert in the storm shutters. "No sense at all." He grunted and shook his head. "Can't see a thing," he muttered. "Wonder how deep the water is."

I looked up at the twelve-foot walls of the kitchen. "What I'm wondering is just how much did A.D. remodel this place? I mean, did he do extensive remodeling? Foundation? Walls? You know what I mean?"

Leroi shrugged. "Some said he spent a bundle on everything. Others said he just hit it a lick and a promise. Truth probably is that nobody really knows. Why? Something got you worried?"

I considered his question a moment. "No, just wondering. These old houses were built solid anyway, almost solid cypress and oak. In storms like this, it's reassuring to know it will hold up against the worst nature can throw at it."

Leroi patted the tabletop reassuringly. "Yeah. Know what you mean."

Janice came back into the kitchen wearing an oversize tank top. Behind her in the parlor, I spotted Giselle pausing to visit with the Venables. I couldn't help noticing she wore the same green tank top she had worn the day before.

Sally entered the kitchen just as another gust of wind and blast of rain slammed into the house, rattling the storm shutters. "What are you boys up to?" she said brightly.

Leroi kissed her lightly. "Tony was saying how glad he was this old house is built like a castle. Nothing can hurt it."

"Yeah. Solid as a rock."

At that moment, I felt vibrations through the soles of my feet.

With a resounding crack that split the roar of the storm and a groaning shudder that ran through every board in the house, the east veranda collapsed.

Chapter Eleven

All thoughts of the three deaths were forgotten as the house erupted into a cacophany of screams.

We had no idea what kind of damage had occurred. The walls were all standing, no water was pouring through holes in the roof, no wind was whipping through broken windows.

"What do you suppose it was?" Uncle Henry stood with his arm around his wife and a couple of his grandkids.

George had opened a French door on the east side and was peering through one of the glass inserts in the storm door. He looked back at us. "I'm not certain, but I think the veranda fell in. The rain is so heavy, it's hard to tell."

Bailey, his cheeks flushed with drink, growled. "Then open the door and look."

"No." George shook his head. "Too risky. The wind could tear it off."

Bailey turned to Patric. "We need to take a look."

"You heard George. Not right now, Bailey," Patric replied testily. "Wait until the storm lets up some."

Bailey glared at Patric, then gestured to Pa. "What do you think, John Roney?"

Pa sat up on the couch, sipped his can of beer, and glanced around the room slowly. "Don't matter to me. Soon as I take a nap, I'm fixing to teach A.D. how to play poker." He took another long gulp of beer, then leaned back on the couch and closed his eyes.

I stared at him for several seconds, wondering if something was wrong with me for not being embarrassed over my own father's drunken behavior. How could I be embarrassed? He was a stranger, one who stole from me the only two times I had seen him in the last thirty-two years.

"George is right, Bailey," Uncle Henry said. "If it's caved in, there's nothing we can do about it. Let's just keep ourselves safe." He glanced at the overhead lights. "And pray the generator keeps running."

Bailey glared at us. Reluctantly, he returned to the couch and plopped down beside Pa.

I decided this was as good a time as any to talk to Uncle Bailey. I pulled out my small notebook.

Bailey sat on the couch, fuming, glaring at Patric Thibodeaux.

I paused, deciding to resort to a little bribery first. I dug through the ice chest for a Budweiser, then I ambled back into the parlor and offered it to him. "Here you go, Uncle Bailey."

He frowned at me. "We need to look outside," he said stubbornly. "See what the storm did."

With a shrug and a crooked grin, I replied, "You know how it is, Uncle Bailey. Nowhere but Louisiana."

He tried not to grin, but he couldn't hold it in. With a chuckle, he took the beer. "You a good Cajun boy, Tony. Too bad you got to live over in Austin with all them heathen Methodist and Baptist."

With a shrug, I said, "That's the way of things, Uncle Bailey." Beside him, Pa snored softly. "Uncle Bailey, yesterday when you went upstairs, where did you go?"

His grin faded. "What you mean, Tony? Why you ask?"

"Because, we want to find who did this. If we talk about it while it's still fresh in our mind, we'll be able to give the state police all the information they need. You might have seen something that could help us. Understand?"

He belched. "You think me, I did it?"

"No." And I didn't. Truth is, I couldn't imagine anyone in our family committing such heinous crimes, but someone did, and I had to help find him, or her. "All I'm going to do is take notes on what you say and give them to the police. That's all. Now, yesterday, Pa and A.D. went upstairs about two o'clock. Later, you went up. Just tell me what you did and where you went, step by step."

He studied me a moment. "Okay, Tony. I tell you. You good Cajun boy. I go up where your pa and A.D. play poker. I think maybe your pa, he want to drink with me, but A.D. make him play the poker. I go to my room, use toilet, then go back downstairs." He shrugged. "That's all I do."

"What about the money clip? How do you explain that?"

Bailey Thibodeaux was a large man, heavy of bone, once possessing mighty muscles that now had turned to flab. As he tried to answer the question, he seemed to shrivel into a wisp of a man.

"Me, I don't know. When I leave John Roney and A.D., he alive. The money clip, I don't know." He sagged back against the couch, his eyes fixed on the French doors.

Strangely enough, I believed him. I resisted the urge to pursue Patric's allegation that A.D. was Giselle's father. Maybe with someone else, but not with a drunk.

"What about A.D.'s will? Are you in it?"

He cut his eyes at me sharply. For a fleeting moment, I thought I saw a flash of fear in them, but then he was shaking his head. "Me, I don't know nothing about the will. I gots no idea what A.D., he put in there."

I tossed out an open-ended question. "Who do you think might have done all this, Uncle Bailey?"

He turned up the longneck and gulped half a dozen swallows of beer, then shifted his gaze back to the French doors. For several moments, he remained silent, and then he surveyed the parlor. "There be some. A.D., he my brother, but he no good. He always try to steal from family." Slowly nodding, he added, "There be them what like to see him dead."

"Who?"

He grinned up at me, a crooked, sad smile. He shrugged. "I don't know for sure nothing, Tony. Me, I'm just a big drunk. Like your pa." He sagged back on the couch and closed his eyes.

I didn't figure to get any more out of him at the moment, but I made a mental note to come back. If I could get a couple names, maybe it would help.

Heads together, Uncle Henry and Uncle Patric sat on the staircase. The two cousins were deep in discussion. They looked up as I approached. I spoke to Patric. "You mind if I visit with Uncle Henry for a few minutes?"

"*L'oh mon non*. You go right ahead, Tony."

Uncle Henry grinned up at me. "You play police with me now, huh, Tony?"

I felt my ears burn. Nothing can put a person in his place like an old relative who had once changed your diapers. "Well, not much of one, Uncle Henry. I just wanted to have a few notes for the state police. That's all."

He gestured to the stair step at his side. "Sit."

I sat. Uncle Henry was of no help. Long accustomed to hurricanes, he had been busy gathering his family to leave when he heard shouts from inside the house. "That's how I hear that A.D., he be dead. Me, I see nobody go up stairs." He cut his eyes to the storm shutters rattling in their frames. "The storm, it have me plenty scared," he admitted. "Even the bear, he don't scare me that much."

"Me too." I glanced at the outside wall, imagining the storm beyond. "They scare me too. Good thing Giselle came up with you. She pushed Ezeline out of the way just in time."

Uncle Henry frowned. "Giselle? She not come upstairs with me. She already there."

I frowned at him. "You sure, Uncle Henry?"

He tapped his work-roughened fingers against his temple. "What you think? I'm crazy? Sure, I sure. I hear big commotion. When I get up there, Giselle, she be pulling Ezeline away from the bear's claws." He nodded emphatically. "That I be sure of."

But that was impossible. Leroi and I were the first to reach the scene. Only Ezeline was there, fighting the bear. Giselle had to have come up with Uncle Henry. The old man just didn't remember. "I—"

Without warning, the shrieking winds of the storm exploded in our ears. "What the—" I shouted, jerking my head around in an effort to spot the source of the roaring. I figured probably another tree or maybe even some object picked up by the wind had smashed through another window.

A scream cut through the roaring. "Bailey! Close that door!"

Bailey had opened the French doors and pushed the storm door open so he could peer into the violent, swirling winds. That was his first mistake. The second was that he had opened the door that faced into the wind. His third mistake was that he had miscalculated the strength of the winds.

When I spotted him, he was bent almost double, straining to close the storm door against hundred-mile-an-hour winds and rain.

He looked around frantically, fear in his eyes. "Help. George! Henry! Help me here. Somebody help me here."

Even as we dashed across the parlor, a loud crack like a gunshot cut through the screaming. The door, and Uncle Bailey, vanished into the storm.

When I reached the open doorway, I spotted Uncle Bailey in waist-deep water, his arms wrapped around one of the columns that supported the portion of the veranda still in place. A twenty-foot section of the second-floor veranda in front of the French doors had collapsed. It leaned against the house at an angle.

Down the veranda, more shutters were loose, banging against the frames.

"Someone get a rope," Leroi called out.

I searched the crowd for Uncle Henry. "The rope you got for Leroi and me—where is it?"

"It on shelves at bottom of stairs," the old man replied.

"Get us some, but be careful of the water. There's bound to be a strong current through there."

He nodded. "I go."

Bailey screamed into the wind, "Help. Hurry. I don't know how long I can hold on."

Someone grabbed my arm. It was Leroi. "Here." He shoved some sheets into my hands. "I tied them together. They'll help until the rope gets here."

Nodding, I threw out one end of the sheets. "Grab it, Bailey," I shouted.

The wind and rain grabbed the sheets, stringing them out almost parallel to the swirling water, well above Bailey's grasping fingers.

Leroi grabbed the sheet and pulled it in. "I'll go down. We'll hold on until Henry comes back with the rope."

Before I could say wait, hold on, or you're crazy, Leroi, clinging tightly to one end of the sheet, slid down the veranda into the water. Moments later, he had tied the end of the sheet around Bailey. Leroi waved at me. "Let's try to get him up."

We tried to hoist Bailey, but the sheet ripped. Leroi grabbed the floundering man and pulled him back to the column where they both clung desperately.

Behind me, a terrified scream echoed through the house, followed by the slamming of a door and another terrified scream. "Snakes!"

I looked around at Patric. "What's going on now?"

Uncle Henry's voice carried above the storm. "The basement stairs are covered with snakes and alligators."

I rolled my eyes. I should have thought of that. I handed the end of the sheet to Patric. "Hold on tight. I'll be back."

Uncle Henry was leaning against the basement door, his face pale as a new sheet. He had his hand over his heart. "It almost scare me to death. I open the door, and the snakes and gators, they cover the stairs."

I muttered an oath.

Someone shouted, "Bleach!"

I looked around at Giselle. "What?"

"I said, bleach. You know, chlorine bleach. Look, I'm sure we don't have any gasoline in the house here, but I'll bet chlorine bleach would drive the snakes and gators off the stairs at least long enough to grab some rope."

I shook my head. "Why not? Let's do it."

Janice headed for the kitchen, Sally and Giselle upstairs. Moments later the three returned, each with a partially full bottle of bleach, two of which we dumped into an aluminum pot.

I picked up the pot and nodded to Uncle Henry. "Open the door and as soon as I throw this on them, slam it shut. Okay?"

He swallowed hard. "You—You bet."

"Anytime."

He jerked the door open. In the next second, I soaked the stairs with bleach, and immediately, Uncle Henry slammed the door.

"How long do we have to wait?" I asked Giselle.

"Not long. Another few seconds, and they'll be gone."

I gave them more than a few seconds. Finally, I opened the door a crack. I grinned. Giselle had been right once again. The bleach had cleared the stairs.

Slowly, I opened the door. "Now, where's the rope, Uncle Henry?"

He crept up to my shoulder. "See them shelves at the bottom of the stairs? Well, the rope is on them spools on the middle shelves."

I spotted the spools. They were half in, half out of the

water. I guessed the water to be about three, maybe three-and-a half-feet deep. To reach them, I was going to be about thigh-deep in water for three or four steps.

I extended my hand toward the remaining bottle of bleach. "Let me have that in case I need it down there."

So, armed with only a bottle of bleach, I eased down the stairs, grateful for the electricity powering the lights. I don't think I would have had nerve enough to go down below with only a flashlight.

Carrying a spool upstairs was not in my plans. All I wanted to do was grab a loose end and scoot back upstairs where we could unroll it away from the snakes and alligators.

Pausing just before I entered the water, I scanned the room that had once served as the dining room for laborers. Beyond was the old kitchen, and adjacent to the kitchen was the old storeroom.

The current was strong and cold. Suddenly, a chill ran up my spine. Beyond the doorway, a wake broke the surface. It was headed directly for me.

I hurriedly sloshed three or four steps to the shelves, grabbed a loose end of rope, and scurried back up the stairs like a frightened mouse.

Just as I reached the top of the stairs, a six-foot alligator burst out of the water. I slammed the door behind me, shivering at the thought of being the first one to go through that basement after the water receded. No telling what creatures might take up habitat there.

We had to open the door a crack to cut off the rope we needed for Leroi and Bailey. Uncle Henry and Giselle continued to unspool the rope. "No telling what we might need it for," she said. "It doesn't hurt to be ready for whatever might come up."

Pulling Bailey and Leroi from the water was almost anticlimatic, for the rescue went exactly as we planned. We doubled the rope, Bailey slipped it under his arms, and we proceeded to slide him up the veranda. Same with Leroi.

"Think you're a hero, huh?" I slapped Leroi on the back.

"If I hadn't gone after him, you would have."

I grinned at him. "Don't hand me that. I know why you went after him."

Our eyes met. I saw the glitter of amusement in his. "You think so, huh?"

"No. I know so. You think you're pretty sneaky. That was the worst thing you could have done to him."

Leroi glanced at the retreating back of Uncle Bailey. With a grin of smug satisfaction, he replied, "It was, wasn't it? That bigoted old man is going to have to live the rest of his life knowing that a black boy saved his life."

"Not just a black boy," I replied, laughing. "But a nephew."

"Who he has never wanted to admit he had," Leroi added to my remark.

We both laughed. Right then, in the middle of all our troubles, Leroi and I were closer than we had ever been. "Come on," I said. "Let me buy you a beer." I was ready for one. I didn't figure the folks in AA back in Austin would object too much if I went off the wagon for a single beer. The last twenty-four hours seemed like twenty-four months. Maybe they would recognize the warp the last two days had made in the time-continuum.

I knew I was using that as an excuse, but at the moment, I didn't care. We were suspended in the middle of a terrifying world of sound and fury and death. If we made it out, then we could go about putting our lives back together.

The incident had sobered Uncle Bailey, a physiological state he promptly set about altering. "Where's a beer?" were the first words to come out of his mouth.

I paused, peering out into the storm. Great oaks and red maples swayed in the wind. As far as I could see, there was nothing but water. I thought about the generator, wondering how high the water had risen.

"What now?" Leroi asked.

"The generator. We need to check on it."

He gestured to the storm. "In the middle of this? We'd never make it to the shed. Don't sweat it, Cousin. If it goes out, then we'll just sit here in the dark. Now come on. I'm ready for that beer."

"I'm for that." I dumped the water from my boots and followed Leroi.

Chapter Twelve

Everyone around the radio grew silent. After a moment, a few men cursed. Janice spotted me and hurried from the crowd.

"What's going on?"

She shook her head. "I don't know exactly. All I heard was that the hurricane went back offshore."

I stared at her. "You sure?"

She gestured in the direction of the radio. "That's what the weatherman said. What does that mean, Tony? It must be bad because everyone seems upset."

"Well, it might not be all that bad," Leroi volunteered. "The problem is that when it goes back offshore, then it can move up or down the coast."

"Where it was heading," I explained, "was east of us, maybe Baton Rouge, or even New Orleans. Wherever it went, we would be on the west side of the eye."

"That's the good side," she said.

"Yeah. But offshore, she could move west."

A woman's voice sounded behind us. "And still come in right on top of us."

We looked around. It was Giselle. "In fact, if you look outside, you'll notice the wind and rain is slacking off some."

Janice slid her arm under mine. "So, it isn't over yet, is it?"

I led the way back to the kitchen. "Hard to say. She might move on down the coast. We might wake up in the morning and the sun will be out. It's just hard to say."

Opening the back door, I peered through the glass insert in the storm door. Water was in the generator shed. Only about a foot or so, I guessed. That meant we had another three feet to spare before the water reached the generator.

Sally and Leroi came into the kitchen. "You better find some more of that bleach, Giselle," she said, gesturing to the parlor. "George Miller looked out one of the storm doors and said the steps and veranda are covered with all sorts of animals."

Janice gasped. I patted her hand and tried to reassure her. "It's natural. Don't worry. Once the worst is over, the animals will be just as happy to get out of here as we will to see them go."

"You sure?" She looked up at me hopefully.

I nodded. "Bet you wish you were back in Austin, huh?"

"Yes."

"I wish we were both back there." I leaned over and touched my lips to hers.

"Think I'll get me something to snack on," Leroi said.

The others joined in. Janice looked up at me. "You want me to make you a sandwich, Tony?"

"No. You go ahead. I'll be in there after I talk to Aunt Ezeline."

Aunt Ezeline was nervous. At first I figured she was still edgy from her husband's close call, but later I realized I hadn't seen her around the window during our rescue efforts, another puzzling detail.

I explained what I was doing and the fact I just wanted her to tell me what she could remember. She shook her head. "I don't like this, Tony. It make me nervous. I don't know nothing to help."

I laid my hand on hers to reassure her. I truly felt sorry for Aunt Ezeline. She'd worked hard all her life. Her eyes reflected that watery hopelessness that comes from years of not quite making ends meet. Her frazzled hair and ill-fitting dress were mute evidence of too many cheap home perms and too much discount shopping.

"Just relax, Ezeline. Tell me about you and Marie going up to your room yesterday to look at your new blouse."

She frowned at me. "Is that all?"

"Unless there's more. Just tell all about it."

"Not much to say, Tony. I find a blouse at Carpenter's in Eunice. It costs half what one like it costs at the Junior Shop."

"Did you see anyone when you were going up to your room?"

She studied the question. "Leroi," she said. "We see Leroi."

"Anyone else?"

She shook her head. "No."

"Then what?"

"After Marie see the blouse, we come back downstairs."

"Together?"

"*Oui.*"

"You didn't go to A.D.'s room?"

"No."

Remembering Patric's assertion that she had discovered the body, I asked. "Who found A.D.?"

She hesitated. "Me, I don't know. I was downstairs when someone say A.D., he dead." She shook her head. "I never go in room."

I closed my notebook and, with a grin, said, "See? That's all there is to it."

But, as far as I was concerned, that wasn't it. Already stories were contradicting each other.

Next, I visited Kay Miller, Uncle George's daughter, and

after her, a dozen other family members. I came away with nothing.

In the kitchen, Janice handed me a thick ham sandwich and a heaping mound of potato salad. Giving her a light kiss on her cheek, I opened a cold soft drink and plopped down at the table. Leroi and Sally were polishing off their lunch. Giselle was drinking a beer.

I took a large bite and groaned. "I didn't realize I was so hungry."

"Tastes good, huh?" Janice asked.

"And how." I washed the mouthful down with a gulp of Dr. Pepper.

"Well, I hope you like it." She gestured to her oversize tanktop. "I spilled mayonnaise on my shirt making it."

I laughed. "Sorry. What's the storm up to now?"

Giselle grimaced. "Still heading west along the coast."

"Maybe it'll move over into Texas."

"Those Texans are praying it'll come in over here."

"The rain isn't as hard," Leroi said. "You think we need to check the compressor?"

I thought about the alligator down below. "It has plenty of gas."

"I was thinking about the oil."

Sally laid her hand on his arm. "Don't go out there, baby. If the power goes off, it goes off."

The howl of the wind grew fainter, and the rain didn't drum the shutters as hard. "I don't know. I'm not any too anxious. I think your wife is right. Besides, there's alligators down below."

As if to emphasize my reluctance, a gust of rain jolted the house, and the howling wind swept in like a banshee.

"Then maybe we should wait." Leroi laughed nervously.

"Yeah." I nodded. "We should wait."

"Finally," Sally remarked, her voice filled with sarcasm. "I don't care what the family says, you two boys are getting smart."

After I polished off my sandwich and potato salad, I booted up my laptop and began transferring my handwritten scribbling to a file that I would later send to the Lafayette Police Department.

Some modern criminalists scoff at the old-fashioned habit of note taking, but Al Grogan, the top P.I. at Blevins Investigations, taught me the value of the technique.

Handwritten notes on three-by-five cards provide the opportunity to juxtapose evidence to support or refute various theories. Often, a card from one witness will contradict another, providing other avenues of exploration for solid evidence. And many times, the simple movement of a particular card can trigger a different perspective of the situation.

And that's exactly what happened when I laid out the cards under each name. According to Ezeline's story, she and Marie descended the stairs together, contradicting Marie Venable's assertion that she had left Ezeline up in the bedroom.

I reread both cards.

Different scenarios played through my head. Why had Ezeline remained behind—if indeed she had? And why did she tell me she and Marie had come down together? Was it simply a senior moment? Or was she trying to hide something?

On the other hand, Marie's remark, "when I come down, Osmond, he go up," could have meant both Marie and Ezeline.

I decided to find out exactly what she meant.

Pushing back from the kitchen table, I made my way to the parlor where I spotted Marie and her family gathered against the north wall.

She smiled when she saw me approaching. "Hello, Tony," she said, a cheerful smile on her lips. "You got more questions?"

I grinned sheepishly. Uncle Walter and several of her family looked up at me. "Just one, Aunt Marie." I hesitated, wishing she and I were alone. On the other hand, whatever I asked her, she would relate to her family. "You remember when you told me about coming down the stairs yesterday and seeing Ozzy going up?"

"*Oui.* I remember."

"Was anybody with you?"

She frowned, then shook her head. "No. I come down alone."

"Ezeline stayed behind?"

"*Oui.* She straighten suitcase. Bailey, he make big mess of it."

"Then what?"

With a shrug, she gestured to her family. "I come down. We talk, we visit. Not much."

"Giselle said you saw the blood on Pa's shoes?"

Her face paled. She nodded almost imperceptibly. "*Oui.* John Roney, he sleep on couch. I see blood on his shoes, on his hand. So, I go upstairs. Maybe someone be hurt." She pressed her quivering lips together.

I laid my hand on her arm. "You don't have to say any more, Aunt Marie. I got all I needed to know."

My brain swirled with possibilities as I went back to my computer. Ezeline had remained behind. Why? Could it be that Uncle Patric was closer to the truth than I thought? Was Ezeline so driven by her hatred for A.D. that she would commit three murders?

I poured a cup of coffee and plopped down at the kitchen table, reluctantly realizing that there was indeed some logic to the theory that she might be the killer.

Working on the assumption she was after money, A.D.'s to be exact, Ezeline would have realized there were several obstacles before her. So, she set about eliminating them. After A.D., there was Ozzy the son, Iolande the sister, and the only one left between her and the money—Bonni, the thirty-something daughter who had vanished three years ago. Where she was now, no one had an inkling. Dead as far as we knew.

Ezeline's next step was to place the blame on her husband, Bailey. He would be shipped off to the Louisiana State Prison up in Angola, the playground of the South for rapists, murderers, and a various assortment of psychotic criminals.

I was no estate lawyer, but with everyone dead, in prison, or whereabouts unknown except Ezeline, her chances of being appointed executrix of A.D.'s estate appeared mighty solid. Especially with the good-old-boy judicial system in some of the Louisiana parishes, where a barbecued possum and pint of moonshine would buy you a sheriff's job, and a goat and a quart of the liquid fire would put you in the mayor's chair.

Pursing my lips in concentration, I wondered if Ezeline was smart enough to put together such a devious plan. Or was I giving her more credit than she deserved? The screwdriver and the poison, she could handle. But the cottonmouth? I couldn't imagine Aunt Ezeline within twenty feet of a cottonmouth.

Still, there were several pieces of evidence pointing to her. Motive, opportunity, means. What if she had entered the room, saw Pa passed out, maybe A.D. also. She could have driven the screwdriver through his neck, taken his money clip, hid the cash, and put the clip in Bailey's suitcase.

I gazed into space, considering the possibility. It could have happened, I decided. It most definitely could have happened.

And the icing on the cake for Ezeline would be if Bailey were indeed included in A.D.'s will. Of course, I reminded myself, there was still Bonni, wherever she might be.

I shook my head and returned to the transcribing of my notes.

Then I started on Uncle Bailey. I didn't figure him for the killer, yet he had the motive—the same as Ezeline's—the opportunity, and the means. He was more likely to attempt to handle a cottonmouth than his wife, but either could have slipped one into the mansion in a container concealed within his suitcase.

Common sense pointed to the fact that someone would have had to provide the snake. I couldn't imagine either one snaring it on his own. Once off this island, I knew I could probably find whoever sold them the cottonmouth.

Eunice, Louisiana is a small town. Chances were half the population would be well aware of any of its citizens who could fill orders for snakes.

Suddenly, a far-fetched idea hit me. I pulled out my cell phone and, using my data connection kit, hooked it to my laptop. "Now, let's see if all this technology is worth what I paid for it," I muttered, attempting to connect with my server. To my surprise, I connected.

Don't ask me how I managed the feat in the middle of the storm. The computer is still like magic to me. I have no idea how they work or even why they work. What is even more puzzling is that two identical ones with identical software operate differently.

The most logical explanation a computer-challenged individual like me could come up with for that particular phenomenon is goblins. I firmly believe there are goblins disguised as chips in computers. That's why those devious little machines act as they do at times.

Nevertheless, I quickly accessed the website for the city of Eunice, found the chamber of commerce, and in the comment window, informed them that I purchased live snakes for research and my supply was dwindling. I requested any vendors who might be able to supply my needs.

I paused to reread my request. It sounded professional, so I clicked the submit button.

For a moment, I stared at the screen. It was a long shot, but then, sometimes long shots paid off. Mostly, like the lottery, they don't, but even if this one did not, I wouldn't be any worse off than I was now.

I turned my attention back to Uncle Bailey. A longtime

alcoholic, he operated on impulse. I could visualize him driving a screwdriver through his brother's neck in a burst of rage, but there was no way I could see him deliberately and calmly planning three murders. Poor guy, his brain cells couldn't maintain focus long enough to plan one murder. Sometimes they couldn't even stay focused long enough to remember to pop open another beer.

No, whoever pulled off these murders was cool and deliberate, not impulsive. Still, how did the money clip get in Bailey's suitcase? And where was the wad of bills A.D. had wagged under my nose?

I realized then that if I could find the money, I probably had the killer. For a few moments, I gloried in smug satisfaction over my latest theory. Find the money, then find the killer, but the smugness quickly disappeared when I realized that it had taken me several hours to come up with the idea when Al Grogan and probably half the staff back at Blevins' Investigations would have come up with the same theory instantly.

Outside the kitchen window, the storm shutter banged.

A hand touched my shoulder, interrupting my thoughts. I glanced up to see Janice smiling down at me. "Why don't you take a break?" She looked over her shoulder. "I need to talk with you."

I rolled my shoulders to work out the cramps. "Sure. What's up?"

"Not here." She glanced nervously around the kitchen.

"Something wrong?" I pushed back from the table.

She pressed her finger to her lips. "Not here. Come on." She took my hand and led me from the kitchen.

"Hold on," I said, pulling her back to me. "What's so secretive?"

She hastily scanned the parlor, then stretched up on her tiptoes to whisper in my ear. "I think I know who might be the killer."

In record time, I shut down the computer and slipped the disk into my shirt pocket.

Chapter Thirteen

After hearing her words, I would have followed Janice Coffman-Morrison anywhere.

Outside, the wind and rain kept a steady beat against the storm shutters. I crossed my fingers, hoping the storm would continue moving west. Texans were always bragging that everything was larger in their state. Let them have this one. I'd be happy to admit Texas had larger hurricanes than Louisiana.

She led me to a deserted corner of the parlor. I glanced over her shoulder just as Leroi and Sally went into the kitchen. The rest of the family had gathered in clusters in the parlor and library.

"So?" I prompted her. "Who is it? How did you find out?"

A worried frown knit her brow. "It might be nothing, Tony. I don't know."

"What?"

She hesitated, obviously nervous.

"Come on, Janice. Tell me what you know."

Lifting her eyebrows like a naïve child, she said, "Promise you won't get mad."

Nodding emphatically, I replied, "I promise."

"Say it. You won't get mad."

I held my temper, reminding myself that she was in unfamiliar surroundings, dealing with individuals far removed from the country club set. "I promise. I won't get mad."

With a sheepish grin, she whispered, "Well, you know I spilled mayonnaise on my blouse when I made you that sandwich. Later, I went back up to Giselle's room to change into another blouse." She paused and glanced around nervously.

I laid my hand on her arm. "Go on."

Taking a deep breath, she continued. "Well, you remember yesterday, Giselle wore a red tank top?"

"Yeah."

"When I went up to find another blouse, I ran across the red one all wadded up in her suitcase."

"Okay. So, it was dirty."

Her voice dropped lower. "But there were stains on it. Dirty brown stains."

"Brown?" I frowned.

Her cheeks colored. "I might be wrong, but they looked like what I'd guess dry blood would look like. Most of all, they were those little splatters. Remember the splatters of blood on the card table? That's what the spots looked like on her blouse. A kind of spread-out pattern." She hesitated, chewing on her bottom lip.

Her words disturbed me, but I shrugged off her theory. "Probably stuff from the cottonmouth." The cottonmouth that is no longer there, I told myself.

Janice shook her head adamantly. "No. She's still wearing that tank top. The green one."

My ears burned at the persistence in her tone, but I held my temper. I shook my head. My tone was abrupt. "Not Giselle. She has no reason."

Janice took a step back and studied me a moment, then released a long sigh. "I know how much she means to you. I'm just telling you what I saw. I . . . ah, I don't know much about this sort of thing. I don't mean to be pushy. It just looked funny to me."

Suddenly, I felt like a fool, overreacting as I had. I drew her to me and hugged her. "I'm sorry. Sure, I'll take a look, okay? Probably a logical explanation for it all, but I will look into it."

She pulled back and narrowed her eyes. "You don't believe me, do you?"

"Sure I do. It's just that, well, the others have motives, reasons for wanting to see A.D. and the others dead. Giselle doesn't. Just like Leroi doesn't, or me, or you."

Her bottom lip quivered. I drew her to me. "Come on. You did the right thing. And I promise, I'll look into it, okay?" I curled my finger under her chin and tilted her face up to mine. "Okay?"

A tiny, crooked smile curled the edges of her lips. "When?"

I saw the skepticism in her eyes. Reluctantly, I took her arm. "How about now?"

She beamed. "Good."

"Hold it," I whispered when I spotted Giselle coming down the stairs.

Janice caught her breath. "That was close."

"Yeah."

We waited until Giselle disappeared into the kitchen, then hurried up the stairs. We paused outside her room, looked up and down the hall, then quickly entered. I was still uncomfortable, but it would make Janice feel better.

Janice whispered urgently. "There. The suitcase on the bed."

Just as she reached for the suitcase, footsteps sounded in the hall.

We stared at each other, listening to the approaching steps. They stopped at the door.

I pressed my finger to my lips and motioned to the closet. Silently, we slipped inside just as the door opened. We froze, our nerves taut, ready to snap. The steps crossed the room, then paused.

In my mind's eye, I could see Giselle studying the bedroom, staring at the closet in which we were hidden. I held my breath. The silence expanded, burgeoning into a great balloon ready to burst.

There came the sound of the suitcase being opened, then closed and snapped shut. The footsteps then headed back to the door. Moments later, the door clicked shut.

Janice laid her head against my chest and breathed a sigh of relief.

"Hurry," I whispered. "I'll watch the door."

She dug through the suitcase, careful not to disturb the contents. I stood nervously by the door. After a moment, Janice looked at me over her shoulder, a frown knitting her forehead. "It isn't here."

"What?" I hurried to the bed.

She pointed to a corner of the suitcase. "It was wadded up here, covered by these other tank tops," she said, indicating two or three different colored shirts.

"You sure?"

She nodded emphatically. "I saw it, Tony. Honest. It was there. Not fifteen minutes ago."

Now I was puzzled. I knew Janice wasn't imagining the shirt. She was a levelheaded, sensible woman. "You sure it isn't there?"

Quickly she rummaged through the suitcase once again. She shook her head. "No."

I opened the door hurriedly. "Let's go. We can talk about this downstairs."

As we came down the stairs, Giselle came out of the library. At the same time, a frightened voice carried across the parlor. "Oh, no. Dear Lord, oh, no."

Janice and I locked eyes. We knew exactly what had come about. "The storm's coming this way, isn't it?" Her voice was calm and firm, as if she were telling the parking valet to be careful with her Miata convertible.

I hurried across the parlor to the radio. "That's what it sounds like."

"Maybe it's far enough west that it won't be so bad."

"I hope," I replied, stopping at the rear of those crowded around the radio.

Uncle Henry glanced up at me, his craggy face somber. "This side of Cameron," he whispered.

I grimaced.

"Cameron?" Janice looked up at me.

Leroi and Sally stopped by our side. "On the coast," Sally explained. "Near the Texas border."

A puzzled frown wrinkled Janice's forehead. "That's over a hundred miles from here. Why should we worry about that?"

"That's what's so bad about hurricanes," said Leroi. "They revolve counterclockwise. When they hit land, they usually cut back to their right."

Janice's face paled as the understanding of what lay ahead dawned on her. "So, it could still come in here?"

I squeezed her hand. Nothing needed to be said.

Giselle pushed in beside us. "What's she doing now?"

"Coming ashore. This side of Cameron," I muttered.

Uncle Bailey grumbled. "You might know."

There were a few subdued cries and hasty prayers, but Uncle George attempted to put the bad news in perspective. "Look, folks. We're not any worse off than we were earlier. That storm has a hundred miles to go before it reaches us. We've all been through these things before. And we'll go through them again. So just everyone settle back down and wait it out. We're high and dry."

"And we still have plenty of beer," Uncle Bailey said.

In the background, several of the women said hasty prayers for Uncle Bailey.

I forced a grin at Giselle who had joined us. "At least your mom shouldn't get any of this up in Rayne."

A sigh of relief escaped her lips. "Yeah. No rain up in Rayne."

Back in the kitchen, I slipped down in front of the laptop and continued with my notes. Janice, Giselle, Leroi, and

Sally sat at the table with me, involved in their own conversations.

Uncle Bailey stuck his head in the door. "Tony?" I looked up and he nodded for me to come out to him.

He led me to the liquor credenza.

"What's up, Uncle Bailey?" His eyes were clear. He appeared sober.

He grunted. "Nowhere but Louisiana, huh?" He gestured to the house, and I knew he was referring to the storm and the killings.

"Right. Nowhere but Louisiana."

He lowered his voice. "Me, I think about what you and me talk about. I mean, about who might do this bad thing."

I did my best to suppress the sudden surge of excitement coursing through my veins. For whatever reason, he had decided to expound on the implications he had made during our last conversation. I figured silence was my smartest response.

He chugged a couple gulps of beer. "It be true my brother, he steal my part of Papa's money." He paused, a frown wrinkling his forehead. "No, Tony. Not steal. I tell that because I was *l'idiot*. What really happen was he talk me into a deal, and I agree. Not a good deal for me, but I agree. My Ezeline, she say he steal from me, but I say, I sign papers. I as much to blame as my brother." He shook his head. "But not steal."

I nodded. "I understand."

"After you and me talk, I think long and hard. Maybe I be wrong, but there be two here who can thank the Lord A.D. dead." Before I could ask their names, he supplied them. "Walter Venable and Leroi Thibodeaux."

My jaw dropped open. All I could do was gape at him.

Other than Janice, Sally, and Giselle, those were the last names I expected to ever hear. Stammering, the only intelligent word I could manage to choke out was "Huh?"

Half a head taller, Uncle Bailey frowned down at me. In an apologetic tone, he continued. "I don't like to cause no trouble, but someone, they do all this," he said, making a sweeping gesture around the mansion with his arm. "I think we find them. Who knows, maybe they got some other family members in mind. We got to stop them. That's what make me figure I need to tell you what I think."

I glanced around, half expecting several sets of eyes to be focused on us, but no one seemed to be paying attention. "Go on."

He cleared his throat, then gulped down another swallow of beer. "Well, A.D., he make loans to Walter and Leroi when the bank turn them down. That be this last year, maybe two. Now, he come to me just last week. He tell me that he had made up his mind that he would be a partner with Walter and Leroi."

"Walter and Leroi?"

"*Oui*. Walter, he buy more land for sugarcane and rice. Leroi, that where he get money for his last two shops."

I shook my head. "But, A.D. can't do that. He can't just step in and say he wants to be a partner. The only way he can get their property is if they forfeit on the loan."

Bailey shook his large head. "A.D., he be sneaky. He fix contract so if they miss payment or be late, he can call for the remainder of the loan. He tell me that they don't got the money to pay off the loan, so he will become partner to them."

What Uncle Bailey was explaining to me was simple, but somehow, my brain refused to accept it. "Let me get this straight. Walter and Leroi borrowed money from A.D. They agreed if they were late or missed a note, he could call for the rest of the loan to be paid off."

"*Oui*."

"And they agreed? They really agreed to something like that?"

With a shrug, he grunted. "That the only way they get the money. Walter, he owe the bank too much. The way A.D. explained it to me, Leroi couldn't take a loan because his collateral was not worth what he needed. Me, I don't know about that, but A.D., that what he say."

He hesitated, staring hopefully at me, waiting for my reaction. When I remained mute, he spoke up. "Like I say, Tony. Maybe I talk too much, but I tell myself, this is something you should know, that you should tell the police."

I laid my hand on his shoulder. "You did right, Uncle Bailey. From what you say, it. . . ." I caught myself. I didn't want to contaminate any of his evidence by telling him what I thought, so I simply nodded again and repeated myself. "You did right."

A grin popped on his bloated face. "Good." He hesitated. A frown wrinkled his forehead. "Don't think I tell you this about Leroi because I don't care for him. That gots nothing to do with it." He cleared his throat. "Leroi, he come down in the water to help me. I don't like to hurt him." He hesitated, his face screwed up in concentration. "He is good boy, good boy even if he. . . ." His words faded away, and he gave me a sheepish grin. "I don't mean it like that. All these years, they be hard to change an old drunk like me. But. . . . You understand, Tony? We brought up one way. It be hard to change, but I try. You understand? Huh?"

I nodded. "I understand."

With a satisfied grunt, he turned and waddled back across the parlor and plopped down beside Pa, who it appeared hadn't moved since early morning. The only evidence that he was not comatose was the collection of a dozen or so empty Budweiser longnecks on the floor beside the couch.

Unseeing, my eyes remained fixed on Uncle Bailey while I digested the information he had given me. There was no way to verify it at the moment, but if it were true, then that provided both Leroi and Walter with motives. Each would gain from A.D.'s death.

I grimaced. Not Leroi. He couldn't have murdered A.D. And Walter did not go upstairs. His wife did, but I couldn't bring myself to believe Marie Venable had committed the murder. Still, the motive was there, and both Leroi and Marie had gone upstairs during the window of time in which A.D.'s murder took place.

The voices from the kitchen carried out to me. I didn't want to go back inside. Bailey had given me much to consider.

At this point, there were four family members who not only had the motive, but the opportunity. Bailey, Ezeline, Marie, and Leroi.

Outside, the storm intensified. Earlier than I expected. Abruptly, a shriek ripped through the howling wind and battering rain, followed by a staccato pounding against the wall.

I looked around in time to see one of the storm shutters flapping wildly in the wind, ripped from one of its hinges. Moments later, the second hinge snapped, and the shutter disappeared into the storm.

Loud shouting rose up, but Uncle George's voice carried above it from the stairs. "All of you, sit down and be quiet. We're taking care of it."

We turned as one to see him marching across the parlor with a wooden door on his back and a hammer in his hand. We pitched in to help nail the door across the window.

He stepped back in satisfaction. "I figured taking those doors down would come in handy."

The wind howled and raged in the darkness outside. I looked at my watch. Only six in the evening. I'd lost track of time.

Uncle Patric spotted me looking at my watch. He muttered softly, "You know the eye could come in tonight."

I nodded.

He continued. "It come in tonight, we not repair shutters."

He was right. No way any of us would go out on the veranda after dark. "Then we might as well start taking down more doors, don't you think?"

Patric chuckled. "I think so."

* * *

Back in the kitchen, we sat around the table sipping hot coffee. I'd saved my files and shut the laptop down. It was only seven-thirty, but I was exhausted. I smiled weakly at Janice.

She forced a smile, but from the looks of her drawn face and the rings under her eyes, she was about two good breaths away from collapsing.

Leroi and Sally were in no better shape. For the first time, I noticed that Giselle was not around. Probably in the parlor or living room, I guessed. Doing what she could to help the others.

The storm shutter outside the kitchen window started banging.

Leroi shook his head. "Not another one. You think maybe Nanna's voodoo can stop the banging?"

Sally leaned into him with her shoulder. "Stop that voodoo stuff. It's spooky."

He laughed. "Maybe so, but the cottonmouth is still missing."

I remained silent, staring at them, struggling with my own thoughts. He was right. The snake was still missing. Why would the killer go to all the trouble to clean up the room? Why take the snake at all? What was he trying to prove? Or could it possibly be—I shook my head, refusing even to consider the unnatural theory.

Giselle came in and opened the refrigerator door. "Anyone for a sandwich?"

"Not me," I said. "I got no appetite."

Leroi grunted. "The voodoo's got him."

She laughed. "Don't laugh at it. There are some who swear by it." She slid the platter of ham onto the countertop. "Come on. Eat something. It'll perk you up. Sally, you and Janice come over here and fix those guys something to eat. Just count us lucky that we've had electricity the whole time."

For a moment, no one moved, then Janice threw me a

big grin. "Why not? It's better than just sitting around. Come on, Sally. Let's make them a ham-and-cheese deluxe. Forget about the snake and all that voodoo talk."

"Just don't spill mayonnaise on your shirt this time," Giselle said to Janice. "I don't have any more tank tops upstairs."

Janice glanced at me, cut her eyes to Giselle, then quickly returned to preparing our supper.

I glanced at the pantry. I couldn't help wondering about the condition of the corpses in the freezer. Without a word, I rose and entered the pantry. The blankets hung motionless down the sides of the freezer. I toyed with the idea of looking at the bodies, but quickly decided against it.

As I touched the blankets, they moved. Squatting, I placed my hand at the bottom of the blankets and felt cool air escaping.

I looked around the pantry for some means to secure the blankets against the freezer, some string or tape. Keep more of the cold in, which would be essential if the electricity should go off.

There was everything on the pantry shelves except tape or twine. I spotted the broom closet. Brooms and mops hung on all three walls. On one peg was a spool of kite twine. A curtain covered the back wall.

I reached for the twine, but it slipped from my hand and rolled under the curtain. I leaned forward, reaching for the twine with one hand and extending the other against the back wall for support.

Except, there was no support. There was no wall behind the curtain.

With a grunt, I caught myself before falling. Slowly, I moved the curtain aside.

My heart pounded in my chest and my eyes grew wide as the light from the pantry revealed an opening six feet high. Beyond, the dim glow of the light fell on a flight of narrow stairs leading up to the second floor. I breathed in quickly, then retrieved the twine and backed out of the closet. I closed the door silently.

Doing my best to keep the excitement from my voice, I called out to Leroi. "Hey, give me a hand in here, will you?"

He called from the kitchen. "What's up?"

Casually, I replied, "I want to make sure the blankets are tight around the freezer so no cold air can escape."

"Okay."

We wrapped the twine around the freezer several times before tying it. I stepped back. "There. That ought to do it." I deliberately laid the twine on a pantry shelf. I wasn't about to go back in that broom closet until I was all by myself, and I wasn't about to mention it to anyone, not even Janice.

I still had no idea who the killer was, but I had found the way he managed to move about the house without being spotted. And I was firmly convinced that only the two of us knew about the secret staircase.

Chapter Fourteen

The five of us sat around the table sipping rich chicory coffee, subdued, lost in our own thoughts. I studied my cousins. Could it possibly have been one of them? I couldn't bring myself to believe such could be true.

Leroi had the motive if Bailey were right. Even Sally could have carried out the murders to save her own family, to save what she and Leroi had worked so hard to build.

Then there was Giselle. She had no motive, or none that I could see. The only motive might be Patric's assertion that A.D. was her father, and yet even Patric claimed she knew nothing of it. Of course, Janice had found a soiled tank top that she claimed had blood on it, one we had not found when we searched.

"We best hurry up and get out of here," Sally announced as Aunt Marie led her brood into the kitchen. "The others are coming in to eat."

Out in the parlor, we sat on the couch facing the French doors on the east side, the ones from which Uncle Bailey had fallen. I made a conscious effort not to glance in the direction of the kitchen and pantry. Outside, the storm battered at the house.

"I don't see how you can be so accustomed to storms like this," Janice said, gesturing to the families sitting quietly, the kids playing games.

"We aren't," Giselle replied. "I still jump every time the wind howls or a shutter bangs against the wall."

Leroi changed the subject. "You having any luck, Tony? I mean talking to everyone."

I hesitated. "If you mean do I have an idea who did it, no. All I've really done is gather a lot of information for the police. I don't want to be the one who pins this down. Not family."

"But, you did talk to everyone?" I sensed a note of nervousness in his voice.

"Yeah. I think so."

"You didn't talk to me," Giselle said, laughing. "Maybe you should."

"No need." I shook my head. "According to folks in the parlor, they agreed there were six people who went upstairs between two and four yesterday."

Sally slid her arm through Leroi's. "Six?"

"Yeah. Your husband here, Pa, Bailey, Ezeline, A.D., and Marie Venable." I looked at Giselle. "Grandma Ola saw you go in the kitchen, but not upstairs." I kept quiet about the secret stairway.

She shook her head and laughed. "Grandma Ola doesn't miss a thing. Yeah, the hams hadn't been sliced so I had to take care of that. I figured people were going to start coming in, and I didn't want them to butcher up the hams."

I glanced at the kitchen. There was something about the ham, but I couldn't quite put my finger on it.

Sally leaned forward, her shiny black hair falling over her shoulders. "But, Tony, surely you have some idea who is behind all this?"

I held my hands up in frustration. "I can honestly say I haven't the slightest idea." I looked directly at Leroi. "There are those with good reason to see A.D. dead, and there's enough circumstantial evidence around that would probably focus the state police's attention on one or two of the suspects."

Leroi glanced at Sally, then looked back to me. "You're talking about me, huh? The screwdriver?"

All eyes turned to me. I drew a deep breath and released it slowly. "I know you didn't do it, but look at the evidence. First, yeah, the screwdriver; second, A.D. swindled your father out of oil property—"

"But, that was almost forty years ago," Leroi protested.

"I know, but I'll guarantee you, Cuz, they'll jump on that like snake on a frog."

He grimaced. "You're right. So, what else? Or is that it?"

"Well, you were upstairs. You went to the bathroom, but they could suggest that was only an excuse. Instead, you slipped into A.D.'s room, saw Pa passed out, and stabbed A.D."

Sally blurted out, "You can't believe that. Not about Leroi. Why you and him—"

I held up my hand to stem her flood of protest. "Of course I don't. I'm just telling you what the state police are going to see."

Leroi leaned back on the couch. "It doesn't look good, huh?"

I remembered Bailey's assertions. "That isn't all, Leroi."

He leaned forward, frowning. "More? What now?"

"Is it true that A.D. was planning on taking over a piece of your business? Partner or something like that because of a loan?"

Leroi's face looked like someone had hit him in the forehead with a sledgehammer. He stared at me in disbelief.

Sally's eyes popped wide open. She stared at Leroi in stunned bewilderment. "Leroi! You said—"

He jerked his head around and glared at her. His face twisted in irritation. "I know what I said, but I didn't have a choice. I couldn't get the money from the bank. A.D. was my only chance. I had to take it."

Her eyes narrowed. She set her jaw. "Then you lied to me," she said, her tone accusing.

"I just didn't want you to worry. That's all. I knew I could make the payments. And I could have if we hadn't had the fire in number four last month."

"But you didn't make the payment on time, did you? You knew A.D. was waiting for that mistake."

Leroi chewed on his lip, searching for the right words to calm her. He glared at me, his eyes blazing with anger. "You had to go and stick your nose where it doesn't belong, didn't you?"

"It isn't Tony's fault," Sally shot back, her voice rising. "He isn't the one who lied to me. You are." Her voice grew louder, attracting the attention of some of the nearby family members. Tears gathered in her eyes. She jumped to her feet and stared down at him, her tiny fists clutched at her sides. "For twenty years, I've worked at your side. What else have you kept from me? What other lies have you told me?"

Leroi quickly rose and grabbed her by the shoulders. "Calm down, Sally. You're making a scene."

She shook his hands off her shoulders. "I don't care. You took a chance on losing everything we worked for, that I helped you get, and you lied to me about it." Tears streamed down her cheeks.

I sat quietly, biting my tongue and cursing myself for opening my big mouth.

He reached for her again. "Now listen, I—"

Her hand blurred and the crack against his cheek cut through the undercurrent of murmuring around the room. "Don't talk to me." She sobbed, spun on her heel, and raced up the stairs.

Leroi hesitated. He looked at us, shrugged, then hurried after her.

The three of us remained motionless for several moments, stunned by the sudden confrontation.

Giselle broke the silence. "Is that really what happened, Tony?"

I glanced at her. "Huh? Oh, yeah. According to Bailey,

Tony borrowed from A.D. to open his last two shops. A.D. put a clause in the contract that if Leroi were late or missed a payment, the balance could be called in."

"And it happened, huh?"

"Looks that way," I replied, looking up the stairs. "A.D. didn't need the money. He was just greedy. A partnership was just another acquisition, another piece of property."

"Sure wish I had known," she muttered. "I have a little in savings. Not much, but it might have helped."

Janice blew through her lips. "Makes it look bad for Leroi."

Both women looked at me. I couldn't resist a soft chuckle. "Maybe not all that bad. I got a feeling what he's catching from Sally is a heck of a lot worse than he'd get from the cops."

"I suspect you're right." Janice wrinkled her button nose and glanced upstairs.

I continued. "It wasn't just Leroi. Uncle Walter did the same thing. He borrowed from A.D. so he could buy more land for sugarcane and rice."

Giselle's eyes widened. "You're kidding. Uncle Walter?"

"That's what Bailey said."

"And he missed a payment."

I shrugged. "That's what I was told."

Janice spoke up. "But, didn't you say that Walter did not go upstairs? That he couldn't have killed A.D.?"

"Yes, but his wife did. Marie. She went upstairs with Ezeline to look at a blouse. Then she left Ezeline by herself."

"Then Ezeline could have done it," said Giselle.

"Or Aunt Marie." I shook my head. "So you see what I meant when I said, I haven't the slightest idea who's behind all this."

We sat silently, listening to the storm outside. It seemed as if the wind and rain had been pounding at us for months, and I couldn't remember the last time I had not heard storm shutters slamming against the side of the house.

"I don't know about you two," Giselle said, rising and then plopping down in a wingback chair beside the couch. "But I'm going to get some sleep. Or at least try to." She curled up in the chair and laid her head back. "I'm too tired to go upstairs."

"Sounds good to me," I said, lying back on the couch. I slipped my arm around Janice as she lay at my side, her head on my chest. I looked at my watch. Only nine o'clock, but already everyone seemed to be settling down for the night.

I glanced in the direction of the kitchen. As soon as everyone was asleep, I would explore the secret staircase.

The sudden silence awakened me.

Groggy from sleep, I stared at the ceiling over my head, trying to orient myself. Janice slept soundly at my side. Giselle remained curled in her chair.

I looked at the French doors, then I realized the wind and rain had stopped. The night outside was silent.

We were in the eye of the hurricane. The storm was moving faster than we expected.

I looked at my watch. Two o'clock. I muttered an oath. I had slept five hours. So much for exploring the secret stairway.

For several seconds, I lay motionless. We had planned to repair the outside damage during the eye, but not now, not at night. A quick glance at the French doors reaffirmed my decision.

A few murmurs behind me in the parlor reached my ears. I eased Janice from my arm and made my way over to Leroi and his father who were huddled up with Henry and George.

When Leroi saw me, he grinned sheepishly. "Sorry, Cuz. I made a fool out of myself." He offered me his hand.

I took it and pulled him to me. "Forget it," I said, hugging him. "We'll just chalk it up to brain damage."

He laughed and slapped me on the back.

"What's going on?"

Patric looked around. "We're in the eye. George here wants to go out and make as many repairs as we can."

George ran his fingers through his thinning hair. "The second half of the storm will be as bad as the first. Me, I think we should try to do what we can." He nodded to me. "I know Tony, that you think about the animals on the veranda, but maybe we can use the bleach again, at least until we make repairs."

They all looked at me. I wasn't anxious to step out on that veranda, even with bleach. "When I was a kid, *Grand-pere* Moise took me trotlining with him. He especially liked to go after the big catfish when the rivers flooded. Once when the river was far out of its banks, I wanted to go under a bridge, but he said no. He pulled close enough for me to see what was under there. The snakes had no place to go except the bridge. They were so thick in places, I couldn't even see the concrete."

Henry nodded. "*Oui.* That's what I say. We have same here."

"They couldn't be that bad," Uncle George replied.

I arched an eyebrow. "No. Come with me. I want to show you something I spotted just a minute ago." I led the way across the parlor to the French doors across which we had nailed a solid core door after one of the two storm doors blew away. "Take a look." I pointed at the glass at the bottom of the French door. Between it and the remaining storm door lay a tangle of watersnakes, snug and safe from the weather.

Patric cursed. "Kill them."

"No." Leroi stopped him. "They can't bother us there. After the storm passes, they'll leave."

"He's right," I put in. "And I wouldn't be surprised if this whole house wasn't covered with them. That's why our smartest move is to stay put and keep windows and doors closed tight."

Outside, the wind started picking up. A few splatters of rain slammed against the storm shutters.

"She's coming back," Uncle George announced solemnly.

Henry grunted. "The eye, she small."

"That not good," Uncle George muttered.

"At least she's started again," said Patric.

"Good," Henry replied. "Sooner she start, the sooner she be over." He raised his fists over his head. "Come on, Belle. Do your worst. We going to make it through you."

The storm slammed into us from the west, now hurling its battering winds at the other side of the mansion.

Janice and Giselle still slept, a sound, peaceful slumber. They had to be exhausted. I glanced around the parlor and through the door into the library. Everyone seemed to be sleeping.

Moving quietly, I went back into the kitchen and booted my laptop. If anyone came in, I wanted some kind of excuse for being awake.

I cut my eyes toward the pantry. My heart pounded in my chest. As children, we'd heard stories about the secret passages in the old house, and we had searched for them, but not once had it occurred to us to look in the broom closet. In our fertile imaginations, we expected sliding panels or revolving bookcases, not simply a curtain with brooms hanging in front of it.

Scooping a handful of matches from the match holder on the wall, I quickly crossed the pantry and stepped inside the broom closet. I eased past the curtain and through the opening, at the same time closing the door behind me.

The stairway was as dark as the night outside. In a chilling, frightening millisecond, time regressed, carrying me back to my childhood and the horrors lurking deep in my subconscious. My breathing grew rapid. My heart thudded against my chest. *Easy,* I told myself. *Easy. There's nothing here. Take it easy.*

I struck a match against the wall, and the burst of small flame cast a reassuring circle of light on both me and the stairs. See, I told myself. I held the match up, lighting more of the stairs. No ghosts or goblins in here. The glow of the match flame drove the skulking monsters back into the shadows of my imagination, but I knew they were lurking just beyond sight, ready to leap.

Outside, the storm grew stronger.

Slowly I started up the stairs, one at a time, staying on the outside of each step to prevent any squeaking. After several steps I reached a landing, and I spotted what looked like a thin piece of wood about five inches square on the inside wall of the stairwell. I touched it. It moved.

Striking another match, I touched the block again, noting that it pivoted at the top. I pushed it aside and a tiny beam of light shot into the stairwell.

Hastily, I extinguished the match.

The beam of light remained. I peered into it.

Ozzy's room!

I blinked and looked again, this time pressing my eye to the small hole. It was Ozzy's room. The half-eaten ham sandwich was still on the nightstand and beside it was an empty whiskey tumbler. I frowned. Something seemed out of place, but I didn't have time to figure out just what it was.

Pulling my eye from the peephole, I let the tiny wooden door swing shut on the hole. I lit another match. A small passage cut left for four or five feet. Beyond, the stairs continued up to the next floor. I decided to return later to explore the short passage.

Eight or ten steps higher up, I reached another landing, and there I found a second peephole, this one in the wall of A.D.'s bedroom.

A few feet beyond the peephole was another short passage, and, as the one below, it turned left.

My heel caught on a splintered board, and I stumbled to my hands and knees, sending the tiny match into the darkness. On all fours there in the darkness, I muttered a curse. I struck another match.

The flame flared. My heart leaped into my throat. There, less than a foot from my face, was a cottonmouth, his mouth gaping, his fangs glittering in the match light.

I dropped the match and jerked back, clenching my teeth for the burning strike of the serpent. Moments passed. Nothing happened. I strained for any sound, but all I heard was the storm outside.

Sweat poured down my torso. Easing backward, I rose to my feet. At the corner of the passageway, I struck another match. I extended my arm tentatively. The dim flame illumined the gaping mouth of the cottonmouth. I jumped back, but the snake didn't move.

Then I realized I had discovered the missing cottonmouth.

So much for Uncle George's voodoo phantom.

I stepped over the snake and laid my hand on a panel of wood. I gently pushed on one side and it swung open. I stepped into the closet in A.D.'s bedroom.

"So, this is how he did it," I whispered. "Slipped up the back way, killed A.D., then quietly returned to the first floor. That's why no one saw him go up the stairs." And with that epiphany, the list of possible perpetrators instantly doubled, even tripled.

Overhead, the storm pounded the roof.

Backing into the passage, I headed down to Ozzy's room.

Once inside, I studied the layout. Then I spotted what had disturbed me earlier. The whiskey glass.

The whiskey glass holding the drowned cockroaches was missing. I cut my eyes to the second nightstand where an empty tumbler had been. The glass was missing. I nodded. "Yeah. That's what he did. He put that tumbler in the place of the one with the roaches."

But why?

Even I wasn't so dumb as not to recognize the answer

immediately. The roaches had not drowned. They died from poisoning, and the killer wanted to get rid of the glass.

I studied the nightstand. The bottle of Jim Beam had not been moved, only the glass. I nodded slowly. Chances were, that meant the poison had been placed in the glass, not in the bottle of bourbon. But how? Ozzy went upstairs to his room alone. I saw him heading up the stairs when Giselle went into the kitchen.

Could someone have come in from the secret stairway? Could that someone have been Giselle?

Suddenly, the boards in the ceiling creaked. I froze. Someone was up in A.D.'s room.

Chapter Fifteen

Moving as quickly as I dared, I slipped out through the secret door in the back of the closet and eased down the stairs in the darkness, crossing my fingers I wouldn't stumble or fall. As long as the killer had no idea I knew of the stairway, I had an advantage.

But, it's one thing to have an advantage, and quite another to know how to use it.

I slid back in front of the computer just before Uncle Bailey waddled from the parlor into the kitchen, yawning and stretching. "You got coffee made, Tony boy?"

"I could put it on right fast, Uncle Bailey. Just hold your horses."

"I'll be right back. Got to wash my face." He chuckled. "Ezeline says that's the proper way to excuse yourself to go to the toilet."

"Works for me," I said, grinning. I still couldn't force myself to believe he was the killer.

Later, as he sat across the table from me, sipping the black coffee, he cleared his throat. "I feel kind of bad, Tony. You know, because I tell you about Walter and Leroi. Me, I don't want them no trouble, and I don't want you should think I try to put the blame on someone else. That's not it."

"I know, Uncle Bailey. Like I said, I'm just gathering information for the state police. They'll carry out the investigation."

"But, me, I think I look bad since the money clip was found in my suitcase. What you think?"

I shrugged. "Yeah. Some. I am puzzled about the money, though."

He snorted. "Hey, Tony. I don't got the money. You can go look. You can see I tell the truth." He suddenly jumped up from the table. "I tell you what, Tony. You come with me now. We go look through my room. You see I got no money."

I had mixed feelings. On the one hand, I was enough of a snoop that I gained a certain distorted pleasure from prowling through another's belongings, yet I knew this would be a waste of time. Not even Bailey would be dumb enough to hide the money in his room. "That isn't necessary, Bailey. We can look later."

He grabbed my arm, pulling me after him. "No, no. We look now. Come, come."

Reluctantly, I let him drag me across the parlor.

Aunt Ezeline, her hair in disarray, hurried after us when she saw us ascending the stairs. She grabbed Bailey's arm. "Where you go, old man?"

He brushed her aside. "This is man's business, woman. You not interfere."

She looked up at me. "Tony? You tell me."

We were halfway up the stairs to the second floor. Bailey growled over his shoulder, "He can tell you, woman, but it do no good."

"Don't worry, Aunt Ezeline. Bailey just wants to show me through his room."

Her face twisted in fear. "You mean to search his room? Why?"

I tried to calm her. "No big deal. He just wants to prove

he doesn't have the money missing from A.D.'s money clip."

"No." She screeched and dashed ahead of Bailey, throwing herself in front of the door. "No. You don't got to do this. The law say you don't got to say or do nothing that will get you in trouble. You hear me, old man?"

About that time, I was wishing I had not been in the kitchen when Uncle Bailey came in. I think I would have preferred being in the freezer with A.D. than standing here listening to them argue, especially over an issue I had raised.

"Out of the way, woman." He brushed her aside and opened the door. He made a sweeping gesture with his arm. "Okay, Tony. Come see." He picked up his suitcase and plopped it down on the bed. "Come see."

With Ezeline moaning and whining behind us, I half-heartedly fumbled through the suitcase, expecting nothing.

You can imagine my surprise when I came across a wad of hundred-dollar bills thick enough to choke the proverbial horse tucked away in one of his socks.

All Uncle Bailey could do was stare dumbly at the roll of bills while Ezeline wailed and moaned.

The roll contained five thousand, eight hundred dollars. I left it with Grandma Ola, knowing no one in his right mind would try to take it from her.

"Me, I don't think Bailey do it," she whispered to me as she slipped the roll in one of the pockets of her dress. "I believe Ezeline do it before I believe Bailey."

I had to agree with her. I had the distinct feeling Ezeline knew the money was there. No proof, but she sure pitched a hissy fit when she heard we were going to search the room.

And I had no problem accepting the logic behind her murdering A.D., hiding the money, and then revealing the money clip to put blame on her husband. What didn't make sense is if she were bright enough to be so devious, why hide the money in one of his socks? And just as perplexing was her motivation for committing such horrendous acts.

To be honest, I was becoming more and more confused.

Janice was awake. She smiled briefly. "Storm started back up, huh?" When she saw the frown on my face, she added. "I woke up earlier when it was quiet. Was that the eye of the storm?"

"Yeah." I nodded. "That was it."

She stretched, then, dismissing the storm, patted her stomach. "I'm hungry."

Several family members had gathered in the kitchen, drinking coffee and chowing down on anything they could find. Janice opened the refrigerator.

I called to her. "Any ham left?"

She pulled out a plastic platter covered with wrinkled aluminum foil. "That's it," she said, removing the foil and revealing a shoulder bone with only a few chunks of ham clinging to it. "Want me to cut some off for you?"

I stared at the pieces of ham clinging to the bone. An unsettling feeling swept over me, the same feeling I had experienced when Giselle mentioned slicing the ham. A series of strobelike images flashed through my head from the day before.

"Tony!" Janice's voice cut into my thoughts.

"Huh?" I jerked my head up.

She laughed. "You want some ham?"

I shook my head, my hunger suddenly forgotten. "Never mind. Not that much left. Let the kids have it." I reached for my laptop on the cabinet top. "I need to do some work in the parlor," I said. "Won't take long."

She smiled brightly. "I'll be in here."

I hated lying to her. It wasn't work I needed to do, but a quiet spot where I would be undisturbed. The sight of the ham bone had suggested a whole new perspective on the case. And then I remembered a remark Grandma Ola had made, which at this moment did seem rather apropos.

But I had to think.

Before I took a step, I felt a vibration in the wooden floor at my feet. I glanced back at Janice. From the expression on her face, she had felt it also. She frowned at me.

Then the house shuddered, followed by a terrible shriek of splitting timbers. The mansion groaned like something live, and vibrations began once again, as if the house itself were shivering in fear.

Uncle Walter pressed his face to the kitchen door in an effort to peer through the glass insert in the storm door. He shook his head. "Too dark."

No sooner had he looked away from the door than a deafening roar filled the kitchen. The entire house seemed to shake, and the storm door suddenly vanished. The wall beside the door popped and appeared to bend outward. There came a sharp crack, and the wall straightened. Moments later, another roar echoed through the kitchen, followed by a loud splash of water.

For some reason, the sound of the rain against the house grew sharper.

The rain and wind beat at the kitchen door, driving water under it.

Janice screamed. I pulled her to me.

She screamed again. "What's happening? What's happening?"

I shoved her into the dining area and herded the rest of the family from the kitchen. "I don't know, but stay out of here until we find out."

Uncle Walter was shining a flashlight out the window in the kitchen door. He looked around as I approached. "The veranda, she fall over here too," he said, nodding toward the cylindrical white beam struggling to penetrate the silver rain. "See. She isn't there no more."

As I peered into the howling, screaming storm, I couldn't help wondering if it were the wind that had destroyed the veranda or the water eating under the foundation, causing it to collapse and bring down the veranda.

We could handle the wind, but for the first time, I was worried about the mansion. If the coursing water had ripped out a hole beneath one corner of the house, the entire structure could come crashing down.

Janice pushed past me. "Here," she said, kneeling and pressing towels under the door to stem the flow of water. "Someone's going to fall and hurt themselves in here."

"Thanks." I grinned at her, at her commonsense practicality in the middle of a raging storm.

"Look," Janice shouted, pointing to the base of the wall beside the door.

Water seeped out from the base of the wall. I frowned, puzzled, then suddenly realized just what had happened.

"What's wrong?" Uncle Patric paused in the doorway between the kitchen and parlor.

I motioned him to us as I spoke to Walter. "Remember that second noise we heard?" Uncle Walter nodded. I pointed to the section of the interior wall under which water was seeping even faster now. "Part of the brick wall outside must have fallen off. That was that last loud splash. Had to be. Otherwise, we wouldn't be getting this water."

"What?" Patric took another step toward the wall.

"There," I said, pointing out at the water seeping in under the wall. "When the veranda gave way, it pulled down part of the brick wall outside."

Janice leaned against me, wrapping her arms through mine.

Walter let loose with a string of curses. "This whole place, she fall in. Them three in the freezer could just up and float away."

Janice gasped.

I shook my head. Time to lie again. "I don't think so. This old house is pretty solid. I think it'll make it." Then I thought about the three in the freezer.

Leave it to Ozzy, I told myself ruefully, staring down at the water spreading across the kitchen floor. He always managed to talk others into handling any problems that came his way. And there he was now, nice and peaceful, and here we were, battling a Category Three hurricane and trying to keep him from floating away.

Go figure.

The darkness faded slightly as the sun rose, providing us enough light to see the wreckage left by the collapse of the entire veranda along the south side of the house as well as a ten-by-twenty-foot section of brick wall that had fallen.

Patric turned to Uncle George who was studying the wall beside the kitchen door. "What you think? This old house going to fall in?"

George stroked the two-day beard on his angular face. "*Non, cher.*" He laid his hand on the doorjamb. "This house built good. Foundation deep. It stand. It be here when we come back next time," he added. "You wait and see."

I admired his optimism, but questioned his foresight.

Janice and I left my uncles in the kitchen. I crossed the parlor to Grandma Ola and Mom. Grandma Ola was still ensconced on her couch sipping her morning coffee and nibbling at her toast. Mom sat at the opposite end of the couch. Both smiled when they saw us approaching.

I gave them each a light kiss on the cheek. "How was your night?"

Mom said she slept fine despite the weather, but Grandma Ola started complaining about the wind, the rain, the hard couch, and the odors that were beginning to permeate the mansion. If I'd let her, she would have complained for thirty minutes, but I didn't have time.

The ham bone had given me some ideas, and I needed to find a few answers.

Chapter Sixteen

Another blast of rain and wind struck the old house, rattling the windows and banging the shutters.

I cleared my throat. "Hold on, Grandma Ola. Before you keep on fussing, I need you to explain something to me, something you said about A.D. and Iolande."

She clamped her lips shut. Her brows furrowed. I figured she was annoyed because I had stopped her before she had the chance to get all her complaints off her chest.

I read from my small notebook. "Day before yesterday when we were talking about A.D., Iolande, and Ozzy, you said, 'They trash. They belong together.' " I glanced at Mom. "And, Mom, you told her not to say that. You remember?"

Neither answered, so I continued. "What I want to know, Grandma, is what you meant by that. What did they do that prompted you to say that?"

Grandma played dumb, a technique she practiced from time to time over the years when she found herself in a predicament brought on by her acerbic tongue or suspicious mind or simply by her gossipy soul. She shook her head. "Me, I don't say nothing like that, Tony."

"No?" I held my notebook in front of her face and pointed to the words. "Here is exactly what the two of you said. And you went on to say. . . ." I read from my notes.

"I just hope they say plenty rosaries when they was alive. Nobody gots the money to say enough masses for them now they dead."

She glared up at me. I had her nailed, and she knew it. I grinned. She could never resist one of my grins. The twinkle came back into her eyes. "Sometimes I wish you never go off to college, Tony. You think you so smart."

I leaned forward and kissed her forehead. "The only reason I'm so smart is because you and Mom are smart. Most of the men in our family are dumber than tree stumps."

She cackled, and Mom smiled broadly.

I got right back to business. "So, what did they do that prompted you to say that?"

Mom and Grandma put their heads together and whispered.

I glanced at Janice who arched her eyebrows and shrugged.

Mom cleared her throat. I couldn't help noticing the blush on her cheeks. She motioned us closer. "Those things, we don't talk about. It best nobody never know," she said in a whisper.

I whispered back, "You've got to tell me. Things are going on here that I can't figure out. For the sake of the family, tell me what you two are trying so hard to keep secret. If it turns out to signify nothing, I'll forget it."

Grandma Ola and Mom exchanged looks. They glanced at Janice, then Grandma grunted. "Tell the boy."

With a resigned sigh, my mother motioned us even closer. "I don't want no one to hear, you understand?"

"I understand."

Mom glanced back at Grandma Ola, who frowned as if she were having second thoughts, but then she nodded emphatically. Mom took a deep breath. "Your uncle and aunt, they be different than the rest of the family. I think it be the money that make them different. For long time, many years, they go on trips to New Orleans. Maybe other places. But they say they like New Orleans. From what family say, sometimes they take Bonni, sometimes Giselle, sometimes all go. Five year back, about the time you take new job, Tony, something happen. We don't know what, but they take no more trips together. Giselle, she stay down in Rayne where she work in church. The others, they go some, but then Bonni, she leave, A.D. and Iolande, they never find her. They say terrible, hurtful things about Giselle. Giselle, she don't say nothing, but she hurt. Her mama, Affina, she don't do nothing to help the girl."

I suppressed a smile. 'The girl' was thirty-eight years old. I figured I knew why A.D.,took Giselle on the trips, to salve his guilty conscience. Only Patric and I knew, and I would never reveal the secret he had shared with me. "Okay. So they don't take her on trips anymore. I still don't understand all the secrecy."

Grandma Ola set her empty demitasse cup on the end table with a sharp click. "I think you say the boy is smart, Leota. He don't act smart to me, just like all them other men in our family."

Mom shushed Grandma. She turned back to me. With only the patience a mother can muster, she said. "Tony, when you was a boy, you hear talk about Iolande and the kind of person she was. Remember?"

"Yeah." I extended my arm and fluttered my hand. "All us kids joked about it, but we never paid any attention. Truth is, we didn't know what we were talking about back then."

Janice tugged at my arm. I read the question in her wide eyes and nodded. She slowly released her breath and shook her head.

"Maybe you don't then," Mom added. "But you do now. And not just Iolande."

I stared at her, not quite certain I understood her implication.

I can remember professors in my education courses at the University of Texas explaining to all of us wannabe teachers intent on saving the world that if a child didn't want to learn, nothing you could do could force him.

I didn't believe it then. Later, I learned the hard way that was one of the few educational hypotheses that did possess an element of truth, unlike most of the erudite-sounding but substantively challenged theories proposed by educational wizards trying to keep their jobs.

At that moment, I was the unruly child who refused to learn. The meaning behind Mom's words bounced off the concrete wall of denial I had instantly erected. "W—what are you saying?"

In a calm, soft voice, she replied, "I say exactly what you think, boy."

I stammered. "I—Iolande, and—and Bonni?"

Mom and Grandma just looked at me as if they were simply watching the evening news. I knew from their studied silence they were waiting for me to continue.

"And Giselle?"

They continued to look at me.

"What about A.D.? He know about all that stuff?"

Neither of them spoke. Their silence answered my question more emphatically than a brass band. "So, what happened? Five years ago, I mean. You never heard?"

Grandma Ola snorted. "Leota, your boy, he not only dumb, he deaf." She looked at me. "Your mama, she tell you, we don't know. The trips together, they stop. Sometimes, Iolande and A.D., they go, but Bonni don't go. Giselle, she never go. We don't know what happened."

I was speechless. I don't know if it was because of the shocking revelation just revealed to me or the fact I couldn't make myself believe such a lifestyle could belong to someone in my family. Then I remembered the game of blindman's bluff Uncle Patric and I had played. That was exactly what he was trying to tell me.

Numbed, I turned and made my way across the parlor to the couch on which Janice and I had slept the night before. I glanced at the French doors. The snakes still lay curled between the base of the French door and the remaining storm door.

Strange how a person adjusts to that which once was unthinkable. I stared at the snakes, unperturbed, as if it were a normal phenomenon that a tangle of snakes slept next to every French door.

"What do you think, Tony?" Janice lowered her voice and glanced over her shoulder. "Do you really believe that about Giselle and the others?" She shook her head. "I don't. Giselle doesn't seem like that? Does she to you?"

"No." I leaned back against the couch and closed my eyes. "She doesn't, but even if it is true, I don't see any connection between it and the murders. I don't see what it has to do with anything."

"Maybe she hated A.D. and Iolande."

I opened one eye and peered skeptically at her. "For simply not taking her on a trip to New Orleans?"

Janice ducked her head and grinned sheepishly. "Does sound silly, doesn't it?"

Leaning forward, I stared at the floor. "I still can't believe what they're suggesting. I don't know Bonni that well, but Giselle, I've known her all her life. Sure, she's always been a tomboy, but then most country girls are. She's a good, decent person, and one of these days, she'll find the right man."

I started to say more, but at that moment, Leroi emerged from the kitchen. He held his hand up for a high five as he approached. "Hey, Cuz. You staying dry?"

"Get a chair. I want to ask you something."

Janice glanced around. "Where's Sally?"

Leroi nodded to the kitchen as he slid a wingback up to the coffee table in front of us. "Getting us some coffee. She'll be along." He plopped down in the chair just as another wall of rain and blast of wind struck the old house. He shivered. "She's moving faster now. Another few hours, and it'll be over."

"The weather, but not us here. I figure it'll take a couple days to get out after the storm."

Curious, Janice asked, "What about your cars and pick-ups?"

With a half-grin, half-frown, Leroi replied. "I suppose they'll be stuck here until the bridge is repaired. I sure hope it doesn't take too long."

I growled. "If the repairs follow the typical Louisiana efficiency, it'll probably take six months."

"Or a year," Leroi added, his tone thick with sarcasm.

We both laughed.

I changed the subject. "You ever hear anyone talk about A.D. and Iolande taking regular trips to New Orleans?"

He stared at me with a blank look on his face. "Huh?"

"Trips. A.D. and Iolande. You hear of them taking regular trips to New Orleans?"

"Sure. Five or six times a year as I remember. They've done it for the last twenty-five years or so if my memory is right. Why?"

"You ever hear any of the older family members talking about why they were always taking those trips?"

A puzzled frown wrinkled his forehead. "No. Not that I recollect. Not specifically, anyway." He glanced over his shoulder, and a conspiratorial grin played over his lips. He lowered his voice and leaned forward. "But, from the way Pa and the other men laughed and raised their eyebrows when they talked about it around the poker table, I don't figure A.D. and Iolande were going down there just to visit a new church or something." He shook his head. "Hey, Cuz, you know New Orleans. Sin City. City of Debauchery, House of the Rising Sun and all that."

Janice and I exchanged knowing looks.

"Why? What's the deal with these trips?" Leroi leaned back in his chair.

I made an effort to dismiss the question. "Oh, nothing. Mom had mentioned they had taken some trips. I'd forgotten about them, that's all."

Sally came up, carrying a tray with four coffees. She forced a laugh. "Time has just run together for me. I don't know if it's coffee time or not, but the coffee was there, the cups were there, and I was there, so I poured us some."

We welcomed the hot, rich coffee.

Leroi sipped it. "Hey," he exclaimed, his eyes wide. "This stuff is better than toking up."

I looked up at him, surprised.

He chuckled. "A figure of speech, Cuz. A figure of speech."

Sally joined in. "Don't worry, Tony. This man of mine wouldn't be alive today if he messed with that stuff. I'd have seen to that, I guarantee."

Leroi laughed again. "And she would have. Trust me."

Sally turned to Janice. "Tony said your family owned a distillery in Austin."

Flashing a bright smile, Janice replied. "Yes. We. . . ."

My thoughts drifted from their conversation back to the problems at hand. While there was more than ample motive for A.D.'s murder, a motive for Ozzy and Iolande was too nebulous to pin down.

Still, there had to be a connection between the three.

I pondered the trips to New Orleans. I wondered if there were any means by which I could learn more details of the trips. Maybe the connection was in them.

My laptop was still on the kitchen cabinet. Even if I could get out to my server to search for an answer, I didn't figure the battery on my cell phone would last long enough to find that for which I was searching. I had another battery in my Silverado, but no way would I venture beyond these walls until the storm had passed and the water receded, taking with it the creatures camped out on the veranda and steps.

But, if the cell phone could keep power for just a few minutes, I knew to whom I could go for help.

I wanted information on two subjects, the contents of A.D. Thibodeaux's will, and any records of trips to New Orleans by A.D. Thibodeaux and guests. I then hooked my phone to the laptop.

Whenever I found myself in a bind for inaccessible or

impossible to obtain information, I went to the web page of Eddie Dyson, computer whiz, entrepreneur, and at one time, Austin's resident stool pigeon.

A few years earlier, Eddie had left behind the dark corners of sleazy bars and greasy money for the green glow of computers and credit cards. He had pulled onto the fast lane of the information superhighway and was quickly becoming a player in the game.

Any information I couldn't find, he could. There were only two catches if you dealt with Eddie. First, you never asked him how he did it, and second, he only accepted credit cards for payment.

Sometimes his charges were expensive, sometimes reasonable, never cheap. But, failure was not in his vocabulary.

Overhead, the lights flickered, once, twice, then went out. Cries and exclamations filled the darkened room. I blinked against the sudden darkness as my eyes grew accustomed to the shadows cast by the faint light from each of the small squares in the storm shutters.

Uncle Henry grumbled. "Blasted lights. And that does it for the radio too."

Leroi looked around. "The generator couldn't be out of gas already. Why, there was several hundred gallons there."

I glanced down at my laptop and cell phone, our last contacts with the outside world. For a moment, I considered shutting them down to save what charges remained in their batteries in case we should need them in an emergency.

But, I was already hooked up and ready to go. Another minute wouldn't rock the foundations of the world, and even if there were an emergency, no outside aid could come in. We were on our own, cell phone or no cell phone.

At the end of my requests to Eddie, I added a brief message, instructing him to call me precisely at three o'clock that afternoon whether he had the information or not. I added that my cell phone batteries were only minutes from dropping dead.

Crossing my fingers, I sent the message into cyberspace.

Chapter Seventeen

As long as the reassuring glow of the overhead lights filled the house, most of us handled the storm with a fairly casual aplomb. With the darkness, though, a gloomy wariness, a shadowy fear, replaced that nonchalant assurance, despite the dim glow of coal oil lamps and the single Coleman lantern struggling to dispel the shadows filling the cavernous mansion.

Janice and I sat on the couch, staring at the storm beyond the French doors. She had slipped her arms through mine and rested her head on my shoulder. Neither of us spoke, each lost in his own thoughts.

The discovery of the secret stairs had punched holes in my theory that there were only four who could have perpetrated the murders.

On the other hand, each of the four had sound motives and the opportunity, evidence that would carry a lot of weight with the state police. I still couldn't figure why the snake was moved.

I glanced at Leroi, who sat with his wife and his father near the kitchen door. Was Leroi capable of three murders? He had the motive. Money. While he still had to pay off the loan to A.D.'s estate, he wouldn't have to worry about a forced partnership. There was still the oil property from forty years earlier. And he had the opportunity. I could see the screwdriver, the poison, but try as I could, there was no way I could visualize Leroi messing around with a cottonmouth water moccasin.

Then there was Bailey. The hard proof nailed him. Both A.D.'s money clip and money were found in his possession. And he also had the opportunity. He admitted being in the room. Sure, he had been drunk. He could have killed A.D. during a drunken blackout, but three blackouts? That was what bothered me. He was too guilty looking.

A fairly solid circumstantial case could be built against Ezeline Thibodeaux. She hated the life Bailey provided her. She hated A.D. She hated being poor. She hated having to shop in thrift stores. People have killed for less.

She had the opportunity, and she had the motive. If A.D. were dead, maybe her husband would share in his brother's estate. Soon I would know whether or not Bailey was in A.D.'s will. If he were, and Ezeline was behind the murders, she could very well end up with the estate, since the majority of the hard evidence pointed to Bailey.

Then there was Marie Venable. She had gone upstairs, and she could have been frightened enough over the prospect of A.D. taking over part of the farm that she might have killed him. And even poisoned Ozzy. But not the cottonmouth.

Those fat, coppery-black serpents with the ridged back were creatures straight from hell. I couldn't believe any of the suspects would have attempted to murder someone with a cottonmouth.

The only one in our entire family who could handle a cottonmouth was Giselle.

Which surprised no one. When we were kids, she knew more about animals and the woods than any of us. And, I reminded myself, she could have taken the secret stairs to the third floor.

That would have provided her the opportunity. But motive?

I paused, wondering. Patric said she didn't know A.D. was her father. Was he certain she didn't know? Would it be motive enough if she learned the truth, and as a result, killed A.D.? Was a thirty-eight-year-old secret motive enough to kill someone? I didn't think so.

And why Iolande? Unless it was something about the trips. Or Ozzy. Poor idiot Ozzy was no harm to anyone except himself. What possible reason would she have for poisoning him?

I heard someone talking, but I paid no attention. I was too absorbed in my own thoughts. Suddenly, someone shook my arm. "Tony?"

I looked up. "Huh? What?"

It was Uncle Henry. He pointed to my laptop. "Can you find out on that thing what the storm is doing?"

My first impulse was to refuse. I wanted to save the battery, but on second thought, I agreed. "Sure. Let's take a look."

After a few minutes of searching, we found a weather station in Florida that was maintaining the status of the hurricane. As we had expected, the eye had moved past and was quickly disintegrating. The storm cut west of Baton Rouge, leaving behind fifteen to twenty inches of rain and thousands of snapped trees, downed power lines, smashed homes, and flooded cities.

From the graphics, it appeared the last of the rain bands should move north of us by midnight.

Several of the younger children had gathered around the laptop, the only display of graphics in the house. Accustomed to a daily dose of video, going cold turkey was hard for them. "Can't you leave it on?" one asked as I started shutting down.

"He can't, dummy," another said. "He's on battery. It'll run down and then we'll really be stuck."

I slipped the cell phone in my pocket. I didn't want to take a chance on one of those video-starved youngsters going online and running the batteries down. For a moment,

I considered removing the laptop battery, but decided against it. I shut the machine down and placed it on the end table.

"Back in a minute," Leroi said, rising. "I see Pa over there."

I grunted and leaned back on the couch, glad for the opportunity to run back over the information I had compiled, hoping that perhaps I might stumble onto a piece I had overlooked.

Sally and Janice continued their conversation.

I glanced up the stairs. On impulse I rose and borrowed the flashlight from Uncle Henry. I wanted to take another look at Ozzy and A.D.'s rooms.

I had no idea what I was looking for. I had thoroughly photographed the rooms earlier, covering every angle, but on the theory that something is always overlooked, I wanted to make another effort. Perhaps I had seen something that was innocuous at the time, but pertinent now.

Perhaps.

I'd been in A.D.'s room maybe five minutes when I heard the creak beyond the wall. Before I discovered the secret stairwell, I would have discounted the noise as old house settling or the wind shoving it around, but now, a third possibility had arisen.

Someone could be watching though the hole in the wall.

I resisted the impulse to make a mad dash for the hidden door in the closet. I knew by the time I reached the closet, whoever was in the passageway would be back down in the kitchen and into the parlor. Plus I would be giving away the one advantage I held by knowing of the secret passage.

Another blast of wind rocked the old house. The walls creaked. I grinned sheepishly and shook my head. My imagination was running away with me.

I took my time, going over the room, taking care to avoid the smeared spatters on the poker table and the dried blood on the floor. I focused the beam of light on A.D.'s expensive luggage. Memories flooded back.

Uncle A.D. had always made an effort to be larger than life, louder than life, and more daring than life. When we were just kids, Leroi and I looked on in envy as he constantly displayed his wealth with expensive boots, fancy stitched western suits, flamboyant automobiles, and an ostentatious mansion too big for anyone except for his ego or a herd of Louisiana Brahmas.

Strangely enough, I couldn't help feeling sorry for him. I swept the beam of light back toward the door, then hesitated. I eased the beam back, settling on a slip of paper on the floor.

Had it been there earlier? I didn't remember seeing it. I started to reach for it, but I remembered the eyes watching me. I'd come back later.

The hair on the back of my neck prickled when I heard the creak again. I spoke loudly enough to be heard through the wall. "Nothing here. I'll try Ozzy's room."

An idea struck me as I left A.D.'s room—a crazy, idiotic idea, the kind you see in the movies. The creaking might have been just my imagination, but I decided if I were going to make a fool of myself, I might as well do it up right. After all, I'd be the only one who would know.

I studied Ozzy's room carefully, making a show of leaning close to the empty whiskey glass and bottle of bourbon and shining the beam of light on them closely.

Taking my time, I pored over the room. Nothing, but I didn't let whoever was watching know. Keeping my back to the peephole, I focused the beam on the floor at my feet. "Umm," I muttered. Then I uttered what I hoped would be the *coup de grace*. "What do you know."

I squatted. "Sure didn't see that before," I said, staring at the round beam on the floor. "Could be important." I pulled my handkerchief from my pocket and made a show of picking up an object. I leaned forward as if to study the item.

Carefully folding the handkerchief, I half turned so whoever was behind the wall could see me slip the handkerchief behind the disk in my shirt pocket. "Need to keep this for the police," I muttered.

I resisted the urge to throw myself into the melodrama I had created. But, as I left the room, I couldn't resist patting the pocket in which I had stuffed the handkerchief.

Actually, I didn't know if anyone were really watching, or if it were the storm wreaking havoc with my imagination. After all, three days in the middle of a hurricane with a killer running loose in a house covered with snakes will turn anyone's imagination into an LSD nightmare.

Before heading downstairs, I slipped back up into A.D.'s room and retrieved the slip of paper. I held it under the beam of light. It was a sales slip from Carpenter's Thrift Store, Eunice, Louisiana. One word and a set of figures were scribbled on it. "Blouse, $2.75."

For several seconds, I stared at the sales slip. I didn't remember seeing it when we took the pictures, but I'd have to take another look at the shots. I laid my fingers on the disk in my shirt pocket. Regardless of what the pictures revealed, the presence of the sales slip blew away Ezeline's assertion that she had not been in A.D.'s room.

Now I began to wonder if perhaps behind that sweet, domestic housewife persona crouched a calculating, cold-blooded killer. After all, she could have planted the money clip and the wad of bills herself while poor old Bailey flopped on the couch downstairs and drank himself into a stupor. But then why would she pitch such a fit when she learned I was going to search his room? Simply an act to remove her further from suspicion?

I jammed the slip of paper in my pocket and headed downstairs.

Outside, the howling of the wind and the battering of the rain appeared to be slackening. As I reached the top of the stairs overlooking the parlor, a few beams of gray light had penetrated the dark room.

Sally and Janice were nowhere around. I glanced at my watch. A few minutes until three. Almost time for Eddie to call. I plopped down on the couch and slid the laptop in my lap. Something felt odd about the computer. I couldn't put my finger on it, but the little portable seemed different. Puzzled, I turned it over.

The battery was missing.

On impulse, I glanced around, halfway expecting to spot it on the end table or on the couch, but it was nowhere to be seen. I studied the computer. The safety clip securing the battery had been removed. Someone had deliberately taken the battery. And that someone had not wanted me to contact Eddie Dyson.

Frowning, I scanned the room. Everyone appeared occupied with his own concerns. Whoever had taken the battery could not have known I instructed Eddie to contact me on my cell phone. I grimaced. Whoever? There was no whoever. Leroi was the only one who knew I had made a contact online. I shook my head. I still refused to believe Leroi was behind the three deaths.

With the battery missing, I was positive now that the killer had been watching from the secret passage. How could I force him to reveal himself?

Janice still had not returned. I looked at my watch. Five after three. Eddie was late. I checked to make sure the cell phone was on. "Come on, Eddie," I muttered. "Come on."

Across the parlor, Uncle Bailey, arms slung wide, lay sprawled on a couch. I looked for my father, but he was nowhere to be seen.

Beyond the couch, several youngsters stood on tiptoe, peering through the glass insert in one of the storm doors.

A ray of sunlight shot through the insert, painting a small square on the wooden floor. Cheers erupted from the youngsters.

The sudden ringing of the cell phone startled me. I fumbled for it. "Yeah. Eddie?" He was breaking up so I moved closer to an outside wall. The reception improved from garbled blurping to irregular static. "You find the stuff?"

"Naturally. What do you want first, the will or the New Orleans trips?"

"The will. Was it hard to get it?"

He chuckled. "Piece of cake. That Bailey Thibodeaux you mentioned. He's in it. The old man's two kids get most of it. This Bailey guy gets a hundred G's. Some broad named Iolande Thibodeaux gets a quarter of a million. There's a survivor clause saying whoever is left ends up with it all." He paused. "Got it?"

My head reeled from the implications of the information. "Yeah. What about the other?"

"I don't know if it's what you want, but here it is. I found records of trips for only the last five years. Hope that's enough." He proceeded to provide dates and destinations for the trips. For the most part, the details were what I expected to hear, until he threw me for the proverbial loop. "Next week, that dude named in the will, Bailey?"

"What about him?"

"Well, him and a woman named . . . ah, Ezeline? Anyway, they have a trip booked to New Orleans, and then from there, to Orlando, Florida."

I hesitated, surprised. The information blew my little Ezeline theory out the window. Unless—I had a thought. Could she have been devious enough to set up the trip with Bailey while at the same time planning to blame A.D.'s murder on him?

"Tony! You still there?"

Eddie's voice jerked me back to the present. "Yeah. Sorry."

"You heard what I said?"

"Yeah. Yeah, Eddie. I heard. That's him. Ezeline is his wife. That all?"

If I thought he had tossed me a neat little puzzle before, he now tied me up with a dandy Gordian knot.

"One more. Same place as the others. New Orleans. Next month. The Paramount Hotel. One of them is named in the will. Bonni Thibodeaux. The other is someone named Giselle Melancon."

Bonni? Giselle?

I was stunned. Before I had a chance to question him further, my phone shut off. The battery was dead.

All I could do was gape at my cell phone. Bonni and Giselle?

The bark of the cornel tree grew tighter in the knot.

To solve his problem, Alexander the Great had slashed the cornel bark knot with his sword. My brain didn't work that fast, but the truth slowly appeared. Like a swamp fog parting to reveal a safe path through the water oaks and bald cypress, the turmoil and confusion of so many bits and pieces tumbling through my head vanished, leaving in their place an unlikely theory that staggered my mind. Yet, dozens of loose ends suddenly had meaning. The ham. The library. The tank tops. The receipt from Carpenter's. Even the money clip and the roll of bills. Now I understood where they fit and what they meant.

Still, a part of me refused to believe what lay before my eyes. A part of me insisted Eddie must have been mistaken.

I stared absently through the insert in the storm door, paying scant attention to the tangles of snakes on the veranda. Even as I stood there, those that had taken refuge between the French door and storm door slithered out.

My hands were shaking. I needed a drink, AA or not.

Chapter Eighteen

I stared blankly at the liquor credenza, at the nearly empty bottles, the dirty glasses stacked on the stained linen doilies.

"Tony?"

I had just picked up a bottle of Jim Beam when I heard the thin, tentative voice. I looked around to see my pa standing in the shadows, John Roney Boudreaux. His wrinkled and smelly clothes hung from his bare bones like a scarecrow. I nodded. "Pa."

He stepped forward into a shaft of sunlight. Though he seemed to emanate a frailty of body and spirit, there was an animal wariness in his eyes, I suppose from the years of bumming around the country, living on handouts or what he could steal.

"Sorry about last year."

"Forget it. I have." But I hadn't. I'd tried to help him, but he had repaid me by stealing some of my personal possessions and hocking them at one of the local pawnshops in Austin. How do you forget something like that?

His eyes focused on the bottle in my hand. He cleared his throat. "I could use a drink."

Suddenly, my desire for a drink, or maybe half a dozen, vanished. "Sure." I squatted and opened the cabinet door for a glass. When I did, a tiny white blossom fluttered out. I ignored it, intent on pouring him a glass of bourbon so he would go back to his couch.

He downed the first one in a single gulp and held out the glass for another, which he promptly sent racing after the first. He drew his bony hand across his mouth. "Your Ma talk to you about me?"

"She said you wanted to come home."

Nodding jerkily, he replied, "I been mighty wrong. But now I think the good Lord is telling me to mend my ways. I'd like to try."

Glancing around, I saw no one was paying any attention to us, especially Mom. Now was my chance to tell him to hit the road, to leave us just as he had thirty-two years ago.

But I couldn't. For some strange, inexplicable reason, the harsh words stuck in my throat. Maybe he was telling the truth this time. Last year, I gave him two chances, and he stole from me both times. I tried to tell myself that maybe, like they say, the third time was a charm, but I knew better. Still, I swallowed my better judgment. "If that's all right with Mom, I don't have a problem." I couldn't believe the words coming from my lips, yet at the same time, I realized that all along I knew that's what I would say.

"You sure, Son? What you think means an awful lot to me."

He was lying. I could see it in his eyes, but then I recognized the truth in Giselle's words, "You only have one father." "I'm sure. It's all right with me." I hated myself for caving in.

He smiled up at me gratefully and extended his glass. I filled it again. He gulped it down and went back to his couch.

I watched after him, my feelings mixed. Slowly, I replaced the bottle. When I did, I spotted the tiny blossom on the floor. I knelt and picked it up. It looked familiar. I rubbed one edge of the blossom between my forefinger and thumb. A thin, yellow film covered my thumb.

I sniffed it. Whatever it was had the smell of carrots. The odor triggered vivid memories. I grimaced and closed my eyes, sagging back against the liquor credenza. Carrots. I remembered the liquor tumbler. I shook my head. Impossible.

But in the back of my head, I wondered if maybe Eddie's information was right all along.

Leroi and Giselle stepped out of the kitchen. I jumped when I saw them appear so suddenly. Leroi mimed surprise. "Hey, Cuz. Didn't mean to scare you."

Giselle glanced at the bottle in my hand. "Is that yours, or can anyone have a drink?"

I joined the laughter, at the same time jamming what remained of the bloom in my pocket with my free hand. "Grab a glass, and I'll pour."

Leroi glanced at the credenza. "Where are the glasses?"

Giselle opened the cabinet door. "In here."

She retrieved three glasses. I poured us stiff drinks, then set mine aside. "Seen Janice?"

Leroi pointed to our couch. "Her and Sally are over there."

Four or five family members, led by Uncle Bailey, gathered around the credenza. Uncle Walter winked at me and nodded to his wife. "Figure with the storm passing over, we deserve to celebrate some."

"Why not? We made it through." I started across the parlor to the couch, my head flooded with concern about my old man and disbelief at who might be behind the murders.

Through the fog in my head, I heard Janice's voice shriek, "Tony! Jump!"

I heard a whirring noise and threw myself backwards an instant before the huge chandelier slammed into the wooden floor, shattering into hundreds of pieces.

I lay motionless. I couldn't feel my left foot. And then a sharp pain raced up my leg.

Moments later, I was surrounded by family. Astonished

murmurs filled the room. Janice was on the verge of tears, and Leroi was urging me not to move in case something was broken. Giselle and Sally were busy feeling my bones to see just what was broken.

"I'm okay," I protested, grimacing against the pain. "It just glanced off my foot."

Then Sally touched my foot, and the pain exploded. She slipped my boot off and gently ran her fingers over my throbbing foot. "Glanced? *L'oh mon non.* Oh, my no. It didn't glance. It broke."

I shook my head. "No. Just bruised. That's all. Help me up. I'll show you."

Despite their protests, I got to my feet. Like Julius Caesar's proclamation, I came, I saw, I conquered. Well, I stood, I stepped, I fell.

The pain was intense. I cursed A.D. for the shoddy workmanship in the house.

Sally nodded to Leroi. "Help him over to the couch. I need to wrap his foot."

"I'll get some bandages." Giselle hurried upstairs.

I clenched my teeth against the pain as Sally worked on me while Janice and the others looked on. Mom leaned over the back of the couch. "Can I help?"

Without looking up, Sally replied, "No, Mrs. Boudreaux. This boy of yours, he'll be just fine."

"Where's Grandma?" I looked up at Mom.

She nodded across the parlor. "She be sleeping. No need to wake her. Sally say you be fine." She patted my arm.

For some reason, I felt a little sorry for myself. Here I was, injured, maybe crippled for life, and my Mom decided Grandma Ola needed her sleep more than I needed sympathy.

On the other hand, maybe it is true that most men are babies when it comes to illnesses or injuries.

I forgot all about feeling sorry for myself when Leroi offered me three fingers of Jim Beam. "Here. This'll help."

I gulped it down. At the next AA meeting, I'd ask forgiveness. *Grand-pere* Moise always chuckled and said that was easier than asking for permission.

At that moment, the entire mansion shuddered. Everyone fell silent in the semi-darkness of the parlor, staring at the walls and ceiling with fear in their eyes. Wood snapped like gunshots. Windows rattled.

The whole place was falling down, just like the chandelier.

Then a rumbling groan, mixed with the snapping of breaking timbers, reverberated through the walls and floors. A violent gust of wind whipped through the house just as a falling wall splashed into the water below.

Uncle George shouted from the kitchen, "The kitchen wall's gone!"

Wind and rain swept into the parlor, and the noises of the storm bounced off every wall in the house. Screams echoed through the shadowy rooms. Someone shouted, "Close the kitchen door!"

The door slammed shut, and an eerie silence followed.

In the excitement, I'd forgotten about my foot, but when I moved it, it reminded me it was broken. I grimaced and fell back on the couch, muttering every curse I could remember.

Sally laid her hand on my arm. "I don't have anything for the pain. Sorry."

"What about some Valium?" Marie Venable smiled down at me.

Ezeline came up to stand beside her. "I have some Darvocet."

At that moment, Leroi brought me another glass of bourbon.

Still addled by the pain, I gave them a silly grin.

My sappy grin broadened when I recognized the irony of the situation. Here I was, looking for a murderer who used poison on one of his victims, and three of my suspects were offering me pills and alcohol. What if one of them were offering me the same poison he gave Ozzy? Whatever the killer gave that idiot cousin of mine sure stopped the pain—forever.

I took the bourbon. I'd already had two glasses, and I wasn't dead. "Thanks. This'll do fine, ladies."

Both smiled down at me sweetly. Marie patted my shoulder. "You're a good boy, Tony. If you need the pills, just let us know."

As they turned away, I spotted Uncle George poking towels around the kitchen door. I squeezed Janice's hand. "Do me a favor. Ask Uncle George if the freezer is all right."

Her eyes grew wide. "I'd forgotten all about that."

"Me too."

She spoke quickly with Uncle George, then hurried back. He looked across the parlor at me and waved.

"He said it was fine," she said, looking down at me. "The kitchen wall from the door to the corner of the pantry caved in, sink and all, but the freezer is still in the pantry. The rain is soaking the floor, though."

I glanced around just as Uncle Patric whispered in Leroi's ear. Leroi gave me a shocked look. By now, the bourbon had started its magical, mystical work, much sooner than in the past. I wasn't surprised. After eight months on the wagon, the body's system is wide open to the devious guiles of wily alcohol.

I nodded for Leroi to come over. "What was that all about?" I asked when he knelt by the couch.

He glanced back at Patric, who nodded briefly. Leroi cleared his throat. "Pa said the ropes holding the chandelier had been cut."

Janice gasped. Sally pressed her fingers to her lips.

I just stared at him, thinking I had misunderstood. "What did you say?"

Slowly, deliberately, he told me again. "Pa said the ropes holding the chandelier had been cut."

That time, I understood. For a moment, a surge of excitement coursed through my veins. That meant the killer had been in the crowd around the liquor credenza.

But, the surge of excitement slowed when I realized that the killer had been after me, and it vanished completely when I realized that all the suspects had been at the credenza along with other family members. There was Bailey, Ezeline, Marie, Leroi, Pa—I shook my head. Pa had already returned to his couch. He couldn't have cut the ropes.

Then there was Walter, Giselle, Sally, Patric, and George. About the only ones not at the credenza were Mom and Grandma Ola. And of course, Nanna, who seemed perfectly content to remain in her wicker chair playing with her voodoo nonsense. For a moment, I thought about the old woman's last remark. "You not find what you want. You find what you do not want."

Her eyes suddenly met mine. I slid my hand in my pocket and closed my fingers around the velvet bag of *gris-gris* she had given me. I looked at the shattered chandelier and wondered. When I looked back at Nanna, she wore a faint smile on her thin lips.

Chapter Nineteen

By evening, the storm had broken apart, but it continued northeast dumping fifteen to twenty inches of rain as it passed.

The sky above us was clear, and a beautiful sunset of orange and purple spread across the heavens. The coal oil lamps filled the house with a sharp, tangy odor that stung the nostrils and burned the eyes.

Most of the water had drained back into the swamp along with the creatures it had displaced. Still, Uncle Walter and Uncle George refused to open the doors. "They still got snakes on the veranda. Come morning, more will go."

So, we were still stuck inside the mansion.

"You think we can get out tomorrow, Tony?"

I looked up at Janice. "Well, we'll be out of the house, that's for sure. I've got an extra cell phone battery in my truck. We'll be able to get something going."

The pain had eased in my foot thanks to the bourbon and the fact I had kept it motionless. I scanned the parlor for Uncle Patric. When I spotted him, I waved him to me. I had to be sure the falling chandelier was no accident.

"Hey, Tony. How you feel?" He looked down at me.

"Good as could be expected, Uncle Patric. Listen, I need a favor. Take a look at the rope again. Was it cut or just untied?"

"It was cut."

"You're sure."

He studied me a moment. "I sure, Tony. But to make you feel better, I look again."

Moments later, he returned. "It be clean cut. Why you ask?"

I wanted to let him in on my plan, but not right then. "Later, I'm going to need your help, Uncle Patric. I'll tell you then."

I watched as he crossed the parlor back to his family. I knew that would be the answer. And it was the last answer I wanted to hear.

Taking a deep breath, I leaned back on the couch.

Janice whispered, "You all right, Tony? The foot?"

I grinned and squeezed her hand. "You've sure hung in there tough the last few days. Sure you're going to want to go back to your daylily shows after all this excitement?"

She smiled brightly. "As fast as I can."

We both laughed.

Her face grew serious. "Now what?"

I glanced at her. "What do you mean?"

She looked deep into my eyes. "You know who did it, don't you?"

Her unexpected question took me by surprise. I hesitated. "I don't know. I think I do, but I just don't know."

She squeezed my hand. "That's because they're family, Tony. That's why you don't know. You don't want to know. I don't blame you."

I studied her a moment, her serious, green eyes, the short brown hair surrounding her oval face. "You think you're pretty smart, don't you?"

She arched an eyebrow provocatively. "Yes."

With a chuckle, I pulled her down and kissed her. "I do too," I whispered.

Leaning back on the couch, I stared at the ceiling thirty feet above us. Taking a deep breath, I decided it was time to test the truth of the often-stated proposition that evidence does not lie; that it cannot be intimidated; that it does not forget; that it doesn't get excited; but that it simply sits and waits to be detected, evaluated, and explained.

At that moment, I could name seven, eight, maybe even nine for whom I had enough evidence to warrant an investigation by the state police. But, as far as I was concerned, of the group, there was only one to whom the preponderance of the evidence, though circumstantial, pointed.

I had to be sure, and I had come up with a plan to nab the killer.

And I hoped I was wrong.

My plan was simple, probably too simple.

First, I'd place one man in A.D.'s room and one in the pantry, behind the freezer.

Then I'd put out word I wanted to look at Ozzy's room again, using as a reason that in the pictures I had taken with the digital camera, there appeared some evidence that might point to the identity of his killer.

If I made that announcement when all the suspects were gathered, then by the time I hobbled up the stairs to the second floor, the killer would be in his place on the secret stairway. He had to know what new evidence I had seen.

Simple.

And probably stupid, I told myself.

Still, I didn't see any other way. Once we were rescued from the island, everyone would get back to his own life. The intensity of the investigation would be blunted because so much of the evidence was circumstantial, able to be contradicted by a variety of explanations once the killer had time to rehearse his alibis.

I had to have hard evidence, and this was the only way I knew to get it. I had no choice but to make the attempt.

This moment seemed to epitomize Brutus's remark in *Julius Caesar* that "there is a tide in the affairs of man, which, taken on the flood, leads on to fortune."

In the Cajun vernacular, "take a shot, *cher*."

I was going to take a shot.

One at a time, Janice sent Uncle Patric, Uncle George, and Uncle Henry to me. I quickly outlined my plan to them, concluding with the caveat, "Maybe this will work, maybe it won't."

None of the three offered me any encouragement that my idea might be successful. In fact, Uncle George rolled his eyes, but still agreed to help.

George, I stationed in A.D.'s room. Patric and I would be in Ozzy's room. I placed Uncle Henry behind the freezer, reminding him to duck out of sight if anyone came into the pantry.

"Then what?"

I cautioned him, "You're the one who starts the ball rolling, Uncle Henry. You see, there is a secret stairway in the back of the broom closet. If the killer comes in, he'll go into the closet."

"What about you? Where you be?"

"In Ozzy's room. You'll hear me. I'll slam the door."

He nodded. "What do I do?"

"Give the killer a little time to get upstairs. Then leave the pantry and slam the door after you. When we hear the door slam, that's when we'll move into action. There are three ways to exit the stairway. We'll catch the killer at one of them."

By now, dusk had filtered into the house, casting shadows across the ceilings and draping them down the walls. By now, the coal oil lamps were lit, putting out faint yellow balls of light in the encroaching darkness.

I whispered to Janice, "Wait here."

She forced a smile. "I hope it works. You do have your .38, don't you?"

I grimaced. I'd forgotten all about it. Last I'd seen it was when I put it on the kitchen cabinet two days earlier. "No." But I quickly reassured her. "Don't worry. There won't be a need for it."

Giving my uncles a nod, I rose and hobbled over to Mom and Grandma Ola. While most eyes were on me, Uncle

George slipped upstairs at the same time Uncle Henry opened the kitchen door a crack and slipped inside. No one seemed to notice.

I hoped.

"You and Grandma Ola doing all right, Mom?"

"Tony. You shouldn't be on that foot."

"It's okay, Mom. I've got some more looking around to do. I wanted to borrow your flashlight."

"Where are you going?" She handed me the light.

"Ozzy's room," I said, speaking loudly enough for the Venables and Thibodeauxs to hear. "I was looking back over the pictures I took, and I spotted something that might be important. I want to take another look at it. From what I can tell from the picture," I added, touching my finger to the disk in my shirt pocket and laying the blarney on thick, "It might tell me who killed Ozzy."

I felt eyes on me. I looked around. Nanna was staring at me. Slowly, she shook her head and rested her fingers on a *gris-gris*. I remembered her warning, *you find what you do not want*. I shivered as a chill seized me. I shrugged it off. I nodded and continued to the stairs.

Leroi stopped me as I hobbled past. "What's up? Need some help?"

I shook my head. "Nope. Your pa offered to help."

Puzzled, Leroi frowned. "Okay." He nodded upstairs. "Where you going?" Behind him, Sally and Giselle looked on.

"Ozzy's room. Remember those pictures we took? Well, I was looking at them again, and I saw something I'd overlooked." I shrugged. "Can't tell, but it might be important." I nodded to his pa. "Give me a hand, Uncle Patric, if you please."

We took our time ascending the stairs. The shadows grew thicker. The hair on the back of my neck tingled when I heard a door creak open down below. I kept my eyes forward.

We paused outside Ozzy's door. The glow of the flashlight beam cast eerie shadows on our faces. "Remember, Uncle Patric. If we hear the door slam downstairs, we head for the closet. Whoever's in the stairway won't have time to be quiet. Uncle Henry will trap them in the pantry. I hope," I added in a whisper.

He nodded. The dim glow of the flashlight accentuated the drawn features on his weathered face. "Do you know who it is?"

"I'm not sure. But if I was the killer, I'd want to know what new evidence has turned up in Ozzy's room, wouldn't you?"

He shrugged and scratched his head. "Hope you be right."

My foot was throbbing. I shifted my weight to my good one. I started to tell him that I also hoped I was right, but the truth was, I didn't want to be right. All I said was, "Okay. Let's go."

We entered the dark room. I flashed the beam over the walls and ceiling, then headed for the nightstand on which the empty whiskey glass and bottle of Jim Beam sat. Uncle Patric slammed the door and came to stand at my side. We stood with our backs to the peephole, playing the beam of light about the top of the nightstand and carrying on a whispered but animated conversation about nothing.

I kept waiting for the slam of a door.

"How long we gots to keep this up?" Patric whispered.

"As long as it takes. Be patient."

We squatted and ran our fingers over the floor at the base of the nightstand.

Suddenly, a door slammed below.

"That's it," I shouted, making a dash for the closet. I hit the back of the closet and the panel popped open.

The clatter of feet echoed up the dark stairway.

I raced down the stairs. Patric was right behind me. Uncle George was behind us. Below, I spotted a shadow. Without warning, I banged my foot into a stud in the wall.

A flash of pain ripped up my leg like a bolt of lightning, and I felt myself tumbling head over heels down the stairs.

I hit the bottom and tried to jump to my feet, but my foot wouldn't hold me. I collapsed. Patric stumbled over me. Then Uncle George fell over me. In the midst of the confusion, I heard a banging on the pantry door.

"There, by the door," I shouted. "The killer." I started to say more, but Patric accidentally stomped on my foot when he leaped to his feet.

I yelped in pain.

With a growl, he lunged at the shadow. Someone shouted, "Hey! What the—"

Canned goods clattered to the floor as the two shadows banged into the pantry shelves.

"I got you now," shouted Patric.

"Leave me alone, you idiot. What do you think—"

"You shut up, you."

Grabbing at each other and shouting, the shadows tumbled to the floor. I managed to climb on top of them. I shouted, "Henry! Hurry. Open the door."

The door burst open. Uncle Henry rushed inside, shining his light on the tangle of arms and legs squirming about on the floor. "You got 'em? You got 'em?"

"Yeah," I muttered between clenched teeth. "Get a light."

Patric grunted. "You betcha I got him. I got him good. He ain't going kill nobody else."

"Well, let him up," shouted Henry, tugging at Patric.

Patric stumbled to his feet, his chest heaving. "Yeah, we got him."

Henry shined the light beam on the prone figure.

Leroi!

Chapter Twenty

"Leroi!" Patric's jaw dropped open. He stammered and stuttered before he managed to get out, "Leroi! What you do here?"

A wave of nausea cramped my stomach. I didn't know if it was from the pain in my foot on which Patric had stomped or the sight of Leroi sprawled on the pantry floor.

"Leroi," was all I could mutter, standing on my good leg. "What—" Some detective I was. I couldn't believe I had been so wrong. In a hundred years, I wouldn't have believed Leroi was the killer. But now—

He rolled to his feet and glared at us. "What do you idiots think you're doing? This ain't no game. Somebody could have been hurt. Why—"

The family had gathered in the kitchen behind Henry. A handful had pushed into the pantry. Patric and Henry exchanged puzzled looks. The beams from several flashlights illuminated the room.

I collected my thoughts. "Hold on, Leroi. That's what we want to know. What were you doing up there? And how did you know about the secret stairway?"

The light beams flashed on his face. He held up his hand to shade his eyes. His voice was sharp with anger. "Hey, Cuz, I could ask you the same thing."

"Yeah, but we're asking you." I limped forward.

Patric cleared his throat. "That's right, Son. What you doing up there? Why you run?"

"You'd run too if people started chasing you down a dark stairway."

His father shook his head. "Why was you up there anyways?"

He looked at his pa, then shifted his gaze to me, then to Henry. "Truth is, you and Pa were acting so secret-like, I got curious. I decided to see what all that new evidence was. That's why."

At that moment, I saw my case falling apart. Maybe I should have stayed at Madison High School teaching English. "How'd you know about the stairs? When we were talking day before yesterday, you said you didn't know about any secret passages."

He shrugged. "That's right. No big deal. Giselle told me about them. We were wondering why you had Pa help you upstairs and not one of us. So I figured I'd see what the new evidence was whether you liked it or not."

"Giselle?"

"Yeah. She said she'd known about the stairway for years."

Hoping I had misunderstood him, I said, "Giselle told you about the stairway?"

She spoke up. "Everybody's known about it for years. I was surprised Leroi hadn't heard of it."

Before I could question her assertion, Leroi broke in. "What did you find up there? I couldn't tell what you were looking at. What was it?"

"Yeah, Tony," Uncle Bailey said from the rear of the crowd. "What is this new evidence?"

Well, Tony, you did it again, I told myself, realizing I had no choice but to admit that the whole thing was a ruse to draw out the killer, who was turning out to be smarter than I thought.

What little new respect I had gained over the last few

days from my family was about to be washed away with laughter at such a hapless attempt on my part.

"What about it, Tony? Where's the new evidence?" Leroi stared at me.

I took a deep breath. "Truth is, folks, there isn't any new evidence."

No one spoke for a moment.

Bailey pushed through the crowd, holding the Coleman lantern over his head. The light was almost blinding. "Don't hold out, Tony. If there was new evidence, tell us. We're entitled to know who's responsible."

"Hey, it's the truth." I nodded to Patric. "Ask him. He'll tell you. There wasn't anything in the room."

Aunt Ezeline grabbed my arm and turned me around to face her. "If you found something that proves my husband didn't do it, then tell me. I've got to know."

Several voices joined in.

"Don't lie to us, Tony."

Mom spun Ezeline around. "Now, you just hush, Ezeline Thibodeaux. If my boy says there's no evidence, then there's no evidence."

"I'm not lying," I shouted over the clamoring of voices. "There's no evidence. I made it up."

An impatient feminine voice retorted, "Oh, no? Then what about the handkerchief in his shirt pocket? What is—"

I cut my eyes to the speaker.

Giselle!

Eyes wide in disbelief at the blunder she had made, she stared at me. Our eyes met.

I knew the truth, and the wild look in her eyes told me she realized I knew.

I tugged the handkerchief an inch or so from my shirt pocket. "This handkerchief?"

She didn't answer. She squinted against the bright light of the Coleman lantern.

I spoke to the family. "The only one who knew about this was the one hiding in the stairway yesterday, the one who used the back stairs to move up to the third floor and kill A.D." The last deduction was quite a reach, but I had to gamble.

Giselle's eyes grew cold. They remained locked on mine. In a casual tone that belied the fury in her eyes, she replied, "I told you. I'm not the only one who knows about the stairway."

Uncle Walter snorted. "Maybe so, but I never knew they was here, and I been around this place nigh on fifty years ever since Marie and me jumped over the broom."

"Me neither," Bailey said. "And I just about grew up here as a kid. I never knew about no secret stairs."

Keeping my eyes fixed on Giselle, I spoke to Bailey. "The entrance is in the broom closet behind me. From it, you can go into either Ozzy's room or A.D.'s. That's how the killer managed to move around without being seen."

I slid my hand in my pocket and pulled out the wilted white flower. I held it up. The flashlights locked on it. "I found this with the whiskey glasses. It looked familiar, but I couldn't place it. Finally, it dawned on me." I extended it toward Giselle. "But, you know what this is, don't you? Water hemlock. Some call it other names. Some call it locoweed. It's poison, and it grows here." I kept my eyes on her. Her eyes grew icy as I continued. "All you do is wipe the flower on the inside of the glass. Leaves a thin film, which the whiskey dissolves. Against the charcoal flavor of good bourbon, it can't be tasted."

"You remember when we were kids, Giselle? Ozzy started to eat a pod, and you stopped him. Me, I would have probably eaten one too I was so dumb. But you knew. Back then you knew."

A murmur of surprise bubbled through the crowd.

Giselle's eyes wavered, then locked on mine again. I nodded to her green tank top. "You've worn that shirt since the first day."

She shrugged. "So?" She glanced at the faces around her, looking for support. "I didn't change. So what?"

"So, you were wearing a red tank top when I got here. When Leroi and I returned from picking up Janice, you'd changed to green."

"I was hot and sweaty. Any crime in that?"

"Then why haven't you changed since? The one you're wearing still has blood on it from that cottonmouth we found in Iolande's room."

She laughed, a short, nervous laugh. "I didn't have any more. I gave them to your girlfriend." Sarcasm laced her words.

Janice blurted out, "Oh, no. You had more. When you gave me one, I saw two clean ones in there. Besides, the red one you had wadded up looked like it had bloodstains on it. That's what I told Tony."

I nodded. "Yeah, but it conveniently disappeared."

Suddenly, I knew where it was. When Janice and I descended the stairs after being in Giselle's room, I had spotted her coming out of the library. I took a wild guess. "Where is the shirt, Giselle? In the library? How about in the clean-out bin under the fireplace hearth where we used to hide secret messages when we were kids? Did you hide it there along with the whiskey glass with the dead cockroaches?"

Without warning, Giselle threw herself backward, at the same time her hand shot under her tank top and pulled out a dark object. My .38.

She fired one shot into the ceiling. "Back! Everyone get back!" She ripped the flashlight from Henry's hand and shoved him from the kitchen into the dining area. "In there. Everyone!" Flashlight in one hand and the .38 in the other, she stood with her back against the doorjamb so she could watch us in the pantry and make sure the others hurried into the parlor.

Women screamed. Some of the men cursed. Janice eased behind me. Leroi sidled toward me. I heard Patric behind us.

I tried to keep my voice calm and level. "Giselle. Give it up. You can't get away with this."

Her head snapped around. She hissed, "Says who? You, Mister Know-It-All Detective. Don't make me laugh. I'm getting out of here, and you'll never find me."

I took a step toward her. "Stop!" She cocked the .38, and I stopped. "You can't shoot us all. There's water all around. What will you do, where will you go?"

She stepped back into the kitchen. I followed, stopping next to a chair in front of the table on which sat a half-empty two-liter bottle of water. She gestured behind her. The full moon shined through the missing wall, bathing us in its cold light. Beyond, the still waters of the Atchafalaya Swamp glittered in the light. "There."

Leroi and Patric came to stand beside me. I felt Leroi's arm against my back as he reached for the bottle. "You'll never make it, Giselle," Leroi said.

She snarled. "I'll make it. In spades."

I pleaded with her. "Let us help, Giselle. We can work through all this."

There was a trace of hysteria in her laughter. "Work through it? How do you work through a family like this? Always laughing behind your back, calling you names? How do you work through a father who never claimed you, but used you for his own pleasure? No, Tony. We won't work through nothing. It's all planned."

All planned?

I remembered the reservations at the Paramount Hotel in New Orleans. I took a wild shot. "Bonni won't be there to meet you, Giselle. That was the information I got today over my cell phone."

She froze. The shadows cast by the moon hid her face. She seemed to shake momentarily.

"You're lying."

"No." I shook my head and drew a deep breath as I made up the biggest lie in my life. "The call was from Lafayette police. Bonni's dead. Car accident. Her and her new husband," I added for good measure.

For a moment, Giselle gaped at me, stunned. "Husband?"

"Now," I shouted, kicking the chair at her and throwing Janice aside.

Leroi shouted and hurled the water bottle just as she pulled the trigger. With a grunt, he staggered back. I leaped for Giselle, catching her around the legs.

She slammed the muzzle of the .38 against the back of my head and squirmed free of my weakening grip.

I blinked up at the moon in time to see her leap from the kitchen to the ground. Behind me, Patric held Leroi. "Get her, Tony," he shouted. "Don't you be letting that one get away."

Janice reached me. "Tony, Tony, Tony. Are you all right? Did she hurt you?"

At that moment, two gunshots exploded from the generator shed. We peered into the darkness. A shadowy figure appeared, dragging a pirogue to the water.

"Let me through, people," shouted Bailey, barging into the kitchen with A.D.'s deer rifle, the same one he had used on the bear two days earlier. He shouted. "Where is that she-witch?"

Patric pointed to the swamp. "Out there."

Bailey stopped at the splintered edge of the floor and squinted into the night. I struggled to my feet beside him, leaning on Janice.

"There she is." He growled.

The black profile of a figure in a pirogue slid across the silvery path laid down by the full moon.

Bailey threw the rifle butt to his shoulder and squinted through the scope.

I hesitated, then whispered, "She's family, Uncle Bailey. She's family."

For several seconds, he remained motionless as the dark silhouette passed in front of the moon and disappeared into the darkness of the swamp, bound for a nearby island.

For several minutes afterward, we stared into the night, each with his own thoughts.

Bailey mumbled, "Nowhere but Louisiana, huh, Tony?"

I laid my hand on his shoulder. "Nowhere but Louisiana, Uncle Bailey."

For the first time I could remember, he didn't laugh.

We turned back to the living room. I heard what sounded like a distant gunshot, but I couldn't be sure. I strained to listen for something more, but all I heard were the sounds of the night.

Chapter Twenty-One

We were awakened next morning by the whup-whup-whup of a helicopter touching down on the lawn outside the mansion. The water had drained, leaving ankle-deep mud. The snakes and nutria had forsaken the veranda. The bobcats, possums, and raccoons had retreated to their trees. The bear was nowhere to be seen, but no one ventured under the house to see if he was there. In fact, no one would dare go into the rooms under the house for a few more days.

Plans were made to move us from the island to a convenience store on the interstate where transportation would be available to take us to a motel in Lafayette after the state police finished with us. From the motel, we would find our ways home.

Leroi was recovering from a neat little hole in his shoulder, Pa was sober, and a general festive mood prevailed throughout the house even as the three deceased family members were carried to waiting helicopters and whisked away to the coroner's office.

"What I want to know, Cuz," Leroi said, lying on the couch, "is how you knew it was her, and not one of us?"

I grinned sheepishly at Janice, who returned my grin. "Truth is, I didn't know for sure. She claimed to have gone into the kitchen to slice ham that first day, but thirty minutes earlier, I'd built myself a ham sandwich. And the hams were already sliced. She used that as an excuse to go up the stairs, slip into A.D.'s room, and kill him."

"What about Ezeline?"

"She was another good candidate. She said she hadn't been in A.D.'s room, but I found a sales slip that proved she had."

"Then what?"

"Ezeline admitted this morning that she had gone into the room and seen the bodies. She was afraid she'd be blamed, so she lied."

Patric grinned crookedly. "Can't say I much blame her."

"No. Don't suppose so. But then there you were. You'd gone upstairs. You had the opportunity. I can imagine what I might do to someone who threatened to take over part of the business I had worked twenty years to build."

"What about Bailey?" Sally asked. "The money clip, the money itself?"

"We'll never know for sure. I'm guessing Giselle did it to throw blame on Bailey. His wife believed he was guilty. That's why she pitched such a fit when we were going upstairs."

"It's a shame about Bonni," Sally said. "I always liked her."

"She isn't dead," I replied, grinning like the proverbial possum. "I had to push Giselle into some sort of reaction. That seemed the best way."

Leroi chuckled. "Maybe you will make a good detective after all."

Janice looped her arm through mine. "As long as it's back in Austin."

We all laughed. "By the way, Leroi. Did you tell Giselle about me contacting Eddie Dyson on the computer?"

He frowned. "Yeah. Why?"

I shook my head. That explained the missing computer battery. "Just trying to fill in a couple blanks, that's all."

"What puzzles me," Sally said. "Is why Giselle moved the snake. Why'd she go to all that trouble?"

"I don't know. The only answer that makes sense to me is she was playing mind games to create some confusion. As you witnessed, some of our twenty-first-century family still believes in voodoo." I shrugged. "And maybe not."

I hoped they asked no more questions, especially about Bonni. Enough family skeletons had been dragged from the closet and cast out in the open for all to see.

Throughout the day, family members were whisked away with promises of a reunion the following year instead of waiting four or five.

Nanna left with Uncle Walter and his family, but not before she fixed me with those filmy blue eyes. Slipping my hand into my pocket and closing my fingers around the bag of *gris-gris*, I remembered her warning. The old lady was right. I found what I didn't want. I pulled out the bag so she could see it. I nodded briefly and pinned it to my lapel. Who knows, maybe there are some things beyond explanation.

One side of her thin lips curled in a smile.

Pa left with Bailey, who insisted Leroi and Sally accompany them. The only way Leroi would go was if his pa went also.

Mom, Grandma Ola, Janice, and I were the last to leave. I gave the police my notes. "Didn't you say you put the information on a laptop?" one officer asked.

I handed him the disk from my pocket. "Yeah. Here's most of it. The rest is on the laptop over there on the end table. I'll get it for you. The battery is missing, though."

"Don't worry, Mister Boudreaux. We'll take care of it and send it to you when we're finished."

I hobbled across the floor to the couch and end table. The laptop was missing. Frowning, I glanced around the empty parlor. "Janice, you see my laptop?"

Mom spoke up. "Oh, don't worry. Your pa took it. He

was afraid you might forget it, so he said he'd keep it for you. He's waiting at the interstate for us."

A warning signal went up.

Later, as we waited in the helicopter, Mom leaned over. "Why did she do it, Tony? She was a good girl."

How should I reply? Should I tell her that A.D. was Giselle's father? Should I tell her that Giselle was part of the rumors revolving around Iolande and Bonni, or that when Bonni inherited the estate, she planned to share it with Giselle? The last was conjecture on my part, but why else would the two of them reserve the wedding suite at the Paramount Hotel in New Orleans? I was no prude, but I didn't even want to imagine what took place on trips when all four went.

Mom shook my arm. "Tony? Tony! You hear what I say?"

"Huh? Oh, yeah, Mom, I heard." In that moment, I decided to let all those skeletons rest in peace. For as long as they would. "I don't know why she did what she did. I guess something just snapped."

Grandma Ola shook her head. "Poor thing. She never know her own pa. Maybe if she had, she be okay now."

I looked around at Grandma Ola.

She looked up at me. "Don't you think so, Tony?"

For a moment, I hesitated, marveling at her compassion, envying her ignorance. "Yeah. Yeah, Grandma. I imagine so."

Janice squeezed my arm.

I looked down at the mansion as we lifted off. I was ready to get back to Austin.

Chapter Twenty-Two

We landed at Parker's Convenience Store on I-10. A chartered bus sat nearby, waiting to take us into Lafayette where we could pick up our rental cars. I looked in the bus for Pa. He was nowhere to be seen.

Don't jump to any conclusions, Tony, I told myself. Maybe he's in the store.

He wasn't.

I questioned the owner. "Yeah. I remember him. Scrawny little bum. He tried to talk me out of a beer, but I didn't go for it. He had one of them laptop computers things he tried to sell me—"

"Great. You have it here?"

He frowned. "No. I got no use for that stuff. He went outside and sold it to a trucker. Come back in and bought a six-pack of Old Milwaukee before hitching a ride east toward New Orleans with another trucker."

I looked down at Janice. A rueful smile played over her lips. She shook her head slowly. I agreed. I should have known.

On the bus ride into Lafayette, Mom leaned across the aisle and whispered. "I don't see your pa."

I skipped the details. "He isn't here, Mom. He won't be. He headed for New Orleans."

She stared at me a moment, nodded briefly, then whispered in Grandma Ola's ear. The two leaned back in their seats, and a small smile flickered across their lips.

By now, we were on the bridge spanning Atchafalaya Swamp at treetop level. From time to time, the trees parted, revealing the dark and mysterious waters of the swamp. Janice laid her head on my shoulder. She stared at the black waters below. "You think they'll ever find her?"

I watched a skein of wood ducks glide down onto a calm stretch of water. "There's almost three thousand square miles of water and forest out there. Even as a little girl, she had a kinship with the Atchafalaya like no one I've ever seen. Will they ever find her?" I shook my head. "Not if she doesn't want to be found."

Two weeks later, word came that Giselle had been found. She had succumbed to snakebite on a nearby island. The medical examiner placed her death on the very night she had fled the mansion. Despite the deterioration of the body, the medical examiner determined she had been subjected to over a hundred bites.

I think about her often, wondering if it could have turned out differently. I don't suppose so. What a shame.

Oh, the snakes. I almost forgot. A week later, I received an e-mail from a snake vendor in Eunice, Louisiana. He could supply me all the cottonmouth water moccasins I wanted. All I had to do was give him a credit card number.

I toyed with the idea of sending one to Leroi just for the heck of it, but I decided against it. I thanked the vendor and informed him I'd just gone out of the snake business.